THE INTERROGATION OF GABRIEL JAMES

BY CHARLIE PRICE

The Interrogation of Gabriel James
Lizard People
Dead Connection

CHARLIE PRICE

THE INTERROGATION OF GABRIEL JAMES

FARRAR STRAUS GIROUX
NEW YORK

Copyright © 2010 by Charlie Price
All rights reserved
Distributed in Canada by D&M Publishers, Inc.
Printed in the United States of America
Designed by Jay Colvin
First edition, 2010
1   3   5   7   9   10   8   6   4   2

www.fsgteen.com

Library of Congress Cataloging-in-Publication Data
Price, Charlie.
    The interrogation of Gabriel James / Charlie Price.— 1st ed.
        p.   cm.
    Summary: As an eyewitness to two murders, a Montana teenager
relates the shocking story behind the crimes in a police interrogation
interspersed with flashbacks.
    ISBN: 978-0-374-33545-8 (alk. paper)
    [1. Murder—Fiction.   2. Criminal investigation—Fiction.
3. Montana—Fiction.]   I. Title.

PZ7.P92477In 2010
[Fic]—dc22

                                                         2009037309

For Bonnie and Paul Swinderman—
magnificent people, magnificent friends

THE INTERROGATION OF
GABRIEL JAMES

Time is simply the yardstick of our separation.
—Ian Caldwell and Dustin Thomason, *The Rule of Four*

1

I STOOD AT THE BACK of a small crowd in a bleak cemetery north of the Yellowstone River, the second funeral I had attended this week. A pastor waited at the head of the grave for someone to offer any last remarks. No one did. The deceased's father stood closest to the coffin, hands cuffed in front of him, long gray hair moving when wind gusted. A deputy sheriff stood beside him, and, farther back, the cuffed man's daughter stood with my mother, both of them in solemn black dresses that didn't look like they would ever be worn for anything but a funeral. There was no music. If there had been any eulogy, I had missed it. I knew other people in the crowd, some from our school, some from the Community Center.

Though last week's warm chinook had cleared snow from the surrounding hills, the ground underfoot was cold and solid, the dust bound by ice. In the distance, clouds drifted southeast toward Hardin and Crow Agency. Other than blasts of wind and people's shoes creaking, it was quiet. Too far from the interstate to hear traffic. Too near the dead of winter for most bird songs. The pastor, a liberal theology teacher from a local college, cleared his throat. "Well," he said, "I guess that's all." It sounded like an apology. Everybody began walking back toward the cars except the father and the deputy.

I stopped to watch, wondering whether the man would throw dirt on the coffin. The deputy took a step back but the father didn't move. He was looking straight out past the grave, out toward the Prior Mountains where a falcon circled above empty rangeland.

Yesterday I had been standing in a different cemetery out the direction he was looking, where they buried another young man. That young man had killed the person being buried today. I knew there was a lot more to the story than that. I knew enough to wish that time could collapse like an old telescope, that some events once seen in greater detail would disappear from the horizon, gone for good. Gone forever.

THE NEXT DAY, Monday, I walked ahead of a deputy sheriff named Childress and a representative from the Billings Police Department into an uncarpeted room in the County Annex.

"We could have done some of this at your house," Childress said. "You're not under arrest."

I waited but she didn't say "yet."

"I'm not exactly . . . I don't want to talk about this at home," I said. The concrete floor smelled stale, the room was too small and too warm. It made my concussion throb.

There were a couple of chairs on one side of the table. I took the single on the other side and noticed my reflection in the wall mirror to my right. I hadn't slept much last night and my face was dull and colorless like a specimen in bio lab. I wasn't sure if I was headed for jail, wasn't sure how much of this was my fault, but I'd come up with a plan. *Just answer their questions. Don't lie, but don't elaborate. Don't let your guard down or give them anything to use against you.* It was a familiar strategy, pretty much the way I'd operated with adults since Dad left.

Childress sat. The Billings police guy stood, leaning against the wall by the door.

"We're recording this," Childress said.

It wasn't a question but I nodded.

She turned on the machine and went through the intro. Introduced the BPD guy as Kosich.

He looked familiar but I couldn't place him. Career Day, maybe.

When Childress finished, she recited the Miranda thing. "Just in case," she said.

I had to say yes, I understood.

"Do you want a lawyer present?" she asked.

"Should I have a lawyer?" I had been hoping this wouldn't be quite so major.

"Do you need one?" she asked.

She didn't ask in a challenging way, didn't put anything into her inflection, but I knew this was an important question. They'd said they just wanted to hear my story. Right. But if I asked for a lawyer wouldn't I seem guilty of something right away? It would be an escalation. But what if I said something stupid and incriminated myself? I had no idea what they could pin on me if they wanted to. I couldn't decide.

"If you want one, it's your right. We'll stop and do this a different way."

I didn't like the sound of that. "I can get one later if I want. Right?"

She nodded.

"Then no, this is okay. For now."

"Why don't you start at the beginning?" she said. She folded her hands on the table between us.

"I'm not sure what the beginning is," I said. It was true. I never caught up with what was happening.

"What do you know about the fire?"

"Not much. I saw it, Anita saw it from the highway when we were driving back the day before school started."

"Anita . . ."

"I don't want to drag her into this."

"You already have."

"Anita Chavez."

The deputy waited.

"She's a junior like me. We go to the same school. At the time she was my girlfriend."

"Driving back. From where?"

"It doesn't matter. What do you guys say? Not relevant."

Childress gave Kosich a long look. Took a deep breath. Waited.

"We'd been camping."

"Just the two of you."

I nodded.

"Overnight?"

I didn't say anything.

"Going to be juniors," she said.

I listened for her disapproval. She spoke so flatly I couldn't tell what she was thinking.

"Your folks know?" she asked.

"They knew we were away for the weekend. Road trip." I wasn't sure whether to say the rest. Guess it wasn't a secret anymore. "They didn't know we were with each other."

Kosich scratched his jaw with his thumb. Other than that, the room was still.

"How did the Ray girl feel about that?" Childress asked.

"I didn't know her then."

"Go on," she said.

"So Anita saw the fire, thought maybe it was a fuel tank at the airport. We got closer and saw it was all along the base of the Rims. I dropped her off—"

"Dropped her . . ."

"At a friend's house to pick up her car."

"And the fire was already started."

"I didn't start the fire."

"And your friend . . ." She paused to pull a small spiral pad out of her shirt pocket and thumb through the first pages until she found what she wanted. "Willoughby . . ."

"Wib. He didn't start the fire either. He fought it. Got the burns trying to save a blue spruce at the side of his property."

She waited.

"Up Cactus Drive at the base of the Rims, the far east side of the fire. He told them that at the hospital."

"He save it?" This from Kosich.

I couldn't tell if he cared or if his question was some incomprehensible strategy of interrogation.

"Yeah."

"Then what?" Childress asked, easing back in her chair, settling in.

"Home," I said. "I figured young kids caused the fire. By accident. Too stupid to burn the big yucca plants and old trees, black the rocks on purpose."

"Didn't you and your friends start a fire near Willoughby's house a couple of years ago?"

How did she know about that? "That was some other kids. We never found out who." My forehead was dripping. I could feel it. I thought she could see it. Great. I've been here one minute and I'm already sweating like a TV crook.

Childress could have been a barrel racer. She was compact, with strong hands that were clean but rough. Her face was similarly weathered, dotted with a few freckles high on her cheeks, and her washed-out blue eyes held me and made me uncomfortable.

"And that night, what did you do?"

"Stayed home."

"Then?"

"I started school the next morning. Saw my friends. Got my classes. Went to cross-country practice in the afternoon."

"Danny Two Bull?"

"That's where I met him."

"And Homer Ray?"

"I didn't know him then."

2

AT SCHOOL MONDAY there'd been constant speculation as to what caused the fire. Cross-country practice started that afternoon and we were still talking about who might have done it when Coach Scofeld walked in with a new kid, new teammate, Danny Two Bull. Because I followed sports statewide, I had heard the name before. With Billings being surrounded by several Indian reservations, none of us should have been surprised by the surname. A couple of the guys laughed at it and had their faces melted shut by Coach Scofeld's glare. Silence followed.

"Danny, have you met any of your teammates before now?" Coach asked.

Danny shook his head no.

"Anybody know Danny?" Coach asked, turning to the team.

Crane raised his hand half-mast. He was our team captain, our fastest runner, and a regular sports encyclopedia. He, Wib, and another guy named Victor were longtime friends of mine.

"Read about him," Crane said.

"And?" Coach asked.

"And . . . I think he won Class B State half-mile, mile, 5,000, and 10,000 last spring for Lodge Grass or some school south of here."

"All right, Crane," Coach said. "Remember the times?"

Everybody could sense Danny's embarrassment and kept their eyes on Crane.

Crane shook his head.

He was lying! He always knew everybody's times. This Two Bull must be pretty good.

Coach looked around now from runner to runner. "His times would have won our Double A section in most events," Coach told us. "We could take State for the first time ever in cross-country. In track we have a chance to rule the roost, topple Missoula off their high horse. Could maybe even go one-two or one-two-three in the mile and two-mile. We don't drop the baton, we could make off with the distance relays, too." Coach was silent for a minute letting that possibility sink in.

"Anyway," he said, bringing us back to the present, "I want you to welcome Danny and be there if he needs some orientation this first couple of weeks."

I HAD DONE THE TWO-MILE on the Billings J.V. track team and now I was running varsity cross-country this fall. At five ten, one-forty, it was my chance to letter in sports. I had never decided whether I really cared about running. Never decided how good a runner I wanted to be or could be. Last spring I usually ran in the middle of the pack. I didn't dog it, but I didn't train particularly hard, didn't take it very seriously. In other words, I didn't puke before, during, or after races. I ran well enough to fit in.

If I thought about my future, I saw myself as an average guy. And beneath that? Okay, I didn't want to go beneath that, but, beneath that, a guy who wished his mom and dad were still married. Beneath that, a guy who hated his dad but wished his dad was still alive. Beneath that? Maybe a guy who knows sooner or later the bottom will fall out of everything he cares about, so don't get too attached to anything or anyone. Keep some distance, don't get hurt. Jog along, enjoy what you can, forget about the rest.

"WHERE'D YOU GO?" Childress was leaning forward, squinting at me.

"Just now? Spaced out, I guess."

"So, Two Bull?" She leaned back again.

There was a permanent crease in her dark gold hair where her cowboy hat usually rested. She had put the Stetson on the table beside her—so she wouldn't forget it when she got up, I imagined. I thought Mom probably knew this deputy, probably worked with her at the Center from time to time. Sheriff deputies or BPD routinely brought people who were acting strange in public to the Center. See if the shelter staff could calm them down and get them back on track. If not, the officers drove the freaked-out to the emergency room for medication.

"Two Bull was pretty quiet. Definitely as good as his clippings. Our first meet, practice meet, was with Laurel that Friday," I said, answering her question.

"What Friday?"

"I don't know. Whenever it was. The end of the first week of school."

LAUREL WAS TOO SMALL to be in our division, but they always had a couple of strong runners and it was a good way to prepare for the regular season. Twelve miles west on I-90, they were familiar with Billings and didn't need to memorize the street names to keep from getting lost on the run. Coach Scofeld had chosen a course that began with an uphill to the Rims, zigzagged on the way back, and finished with a clearly marked circular pattern through Pioneer Park. Coaches and volunteers monitored the runners to ensure fair play.

Laurel's captain was a short, skinny boy named Moody who used to pitch for my Little League team before his family moved. He was fast, well coordinated, and, even though I knew he smoked cigarettes, he never seemed to get tired. He was good competition and might have a chance against Crane's long legs. Nobody said anything about Two Bull. I don't think anybody knew what to expect, since he'd run behind Crane during our practices.

I was toward the back third of the pack so I lost sight of the leaders once the zigzag started. Coach said Crane, Moody, and Two Bull got back to the park at practically the same time, but then the Indian lit an afterburner and sprinted through the rest of the course. Somebody said he let up at the end but still finished first by about ten seconds. Moody complained that "the red kid" must have cheated, but monitors including guys from Laurel had him marked at every checkpoint.

"SO TWO BULL won his first race," I told Childress. "Afterwards he didn't hang around to be congratulated. That didn't make him any friends. But I think he was staying with Donna Plenty Water and her family. And at school he hung with other Indian kids. Except for cross, I never really saw him, didn't talk to him at all. Then."

"How were you involved with the pets?" she asked.

"The missing pets? I wasn't. I didn't know what was going on."

But that wasn't entirely true.

SOMETIME THE FIRST WEEK when school and cross started, Mom had brought it up during dinner.

"You know," she said, "last weekend while you were gone, there was an article in the *Gazette* about pets on the west side of town."

"What about them?" I'd asked.

"Paper said that several families around here between Rimrock Road and the Rims lost their pets recently. Apparently one owner noticed how many signs had been tacked to telephone poles and been put up on the board in Svenson's Market during the last month. When he called some of the people, they had basically the same story. Their dog or cat went missing from their backyard overnight. None of the animals have been found. I thought that was very strange at the time and now, with Sunday's fire in the same area, it makes me wonder."

"How so?" I thought Mom had become more and more of a worrier since Dad left. And I thought she saw too much hardship in her job, too many poor people with too many problems. It was getting her down.

"Oh, maybe it's just some pet ring operating here briefly, snatching animals and moving them to Helena or someplace for resale, like they do with the bicycles," she said, frowning. "I don't know if the poor creatures were pedigreed or anything. But missing pets and arson is sometimes a constellation of events that means someone pretty disturbed is on the loose."

"Do they know for sure the Rims was arson?" I asked. "Well, anyway, you caught me," I said, laughing. "I'm pretty disturbed and I'm pretty loose so I give up . . . except I didn't do it. So, maybe it's just a coincidence. Think what a mess it would be snatching pets. You'd have to feed them, keep them from barking and fighting. Nobody would want to do that for the little money you'd make, and pedigreed dogs might be traceable."

Though Mom nodded, she didn't look relieved. "You're probably right," she said, "but still, let me know if you hear anything around school."

Two days later, the day before our first cross-country meet, Wibby's dog, Sheena, went missing. That morning in school Wib's eyes were red and he couldn't talk about it without leaking tears.

"When I went out to feed her, she wasn't there," he'd said, rubbing at the moisture with his sleeve. "We didn't hear anything last night. There wasn't sign of a fight or anything, and she's never run off before. I think somebody took her."

Wibby lived above Rimrock Road like the others mentioned in the article.

He joined us when Crane and I drove around and looked for her during lunch. And that evening after cross we picked him up and did the same thing, going slow with the windows down and calling her name all over the northwest side of town. Nothing. None of us ever saw Wibby's dog again.

3

I WINCED AFTER I SAID I didn't know anything about the missing pets and then tried to morph my face into a yawn so they wouldn't notice. If I hadn't dismissed my mom's early premonition that something ugly was going on, maybe I could have handled things better. I glanced to see if either of the officers had noticed my reaction and suspected my evasion. Childress continued to calmly sit across from me. Kosich remained standing, expressionless.

"I mean, uh, my friend Wib's dog disappeared," I amended. "Of course I knew about that. The first week of school. We looked but it never showed up. That's all I knew until a few days ago."

"The whole truth," Childress said. Even tone. No menace, but no leeway.

"Well, later, I knew what happened with Danny in the locker room. I was there for that, and I heard what happened at the Plenty Waters', before the Kalispell meet."

"What do you mean you were there?" Kosich said, listening more closely than I thought.

"In the locker room before cross that night, must have been the third or fourth week of school, there was a bad smell coming from Danny's locker. Everybody had these cheesy simple combination locks that were given out at the start of each season. All the managers had a list of the combinations in case someone forgot theirs. For cross-country, our manager, Theo, left the list hanging against the equipment cage where anybody could see it because he had another school job and didn't usually get to the locker room till after everyone was already dressed and out warming up. So the lockers weren't secure, but we'd never had a problem before."

I told them the rest.

I'D BEEN PULLING on my sweats when Danny arrived. He scowled before he even got near his locker. As he opened it, an animal tumbled to the floor at his feet. It stunk something awful. It turned out to be a small dog, looked like some kind of terrier. It must have been dead for at least a week. It was pretty foul and there were maggots and stuff. Shugaart, who had been sitting in front of the locker next to Danny's, threw up. Danny stepped back for a minute, a really blank expression on his face. Then he turned around and went over to the trainers' room and got a couple of the plastic bags we fill with ice when someone has an injury. He came back, picked up the dog using those bags, and carried it out to the parking lot Dumpster. When he returned, he went to the training room for more bags. He checked through his gear and decided to throw away the shorts and socks that had been under the dog. He put those in another plastic bag. When he got back from tossing them, he took his shoes to one of the big sinks and left them in the running water while he sorted through the rest of his stuff. It all smelled.

About that time Coach came in and was standing behind the dressing bench. Danny didn't look at him. "Why don't you take your gear and get some exercise at home tonight, son," Coach said. "We'll clean up the rest of the mess around here and we'll see you tomorrow afternoon."

Danny put his stuff in his gym bag and left without speaking. Coach told everybody near Danny's to clear their lockers. Then he brought a hose in from the trainers' room and washed the area out.

"You guys get dressed and warm up," he said. "I'll be out in a minute."

The place was stone quiet while he worked.

"I'll tell you one thing," Coach said, before most of us had left. "This is going to stop, right now. Police, FBI, whatever it takes. Bank on it." Then he started using the Lysol and we hurried to get out the door.

"AND THE PLENTY WATER INCIDENT?"

Kosich's question knocked me out of the memory.

"I told you. A couple of nights before the Kalispell meet. I guess somebody put a dead pet on Donna Plenty Water's porch. Poured gas on it and lit it. When Donna's mom smelled it she called the fire department. Supposedly Donna got up and saw what it was and called the police, too."

All of us were wondering what Danny would do. Would he move? Quit cross? Go back to the res?

"Nobody knew if the fire had caused any serious damage. Donna didn't show up for first period and Danny didn't come to school until after lunch. He showed for cross, unreadable as usual. Said he was okay and that Donna and her house were okay, but he didn't elaborate. All of us were uncomfortable about asking him more. He warmed up and did pool exercise and then Nordic and weights like this was a normal day. He was real distant. I thought he seemed super angry, but maybe it was just me."

Kosich had a pocketknife and was scraping at his fingernails. He had to weigh at least two-fifty and had the kind of short haircut where old-school barbers shave around your ears.

"Did you or your friends ever go shooting out at the dump? Plink mailboxes? Fire at vehicles?" Childress asked, abruptly switching the subject but still leaning back.

"Shooting. Guns?" *What was this about?* "Hey, the fire, the pets, shooting? I didn't do any of that stuff."

Neither Kosich nor Childress was looking at me. They didn't acknowledge what I'd said.

"No. I don't own a gun," I said.

Childress raised her eyes to mine, still relaxed, maybe not as patient.

"Well, a .22, but I haven't picked it up in a long time."

"How long?"

I shrugged.

"Verbally," she said. "For the recorder."

"I don't know," I said. "A year? Rabbits?" I vaguely remembered going west of town with Wib and Crane. "Just messing around."

Kosich came closer, reached over, and picked up the first from a stack of four notebooks resting on the table between him and Childress. Chose a marked page about a third of the way through. "Heard shooting, guys at the dump," he read. He looked at me. "These are from—"

"Hey," Childress interrupted him. Creased her eyebrows.

Kosich turned away from her slightly, used his finger as a marker to silently read a few more lines. Put the book down and returned the deputy's gaze. Cleared his throat.

I didn't know if that was a communication or a reflex.

"You never killed rats at the landfill?" he asked. "Potted strays? Never associated with the Dersch twins? Partied with Jules and Judd?"

I was shaking my head. "Never did any of that. I didn't know the twins' names till the end."

"Know anybody that shoots cows? Sheep? Cessnas?"

Was he talking about Homer? What were those notebooks?

"I don't know anything about that," I said.

"Really? Not familiar?" Childress asked.

"No," I said, but the denial sounded empty.

One thing that surprised me. Childress had colored some. Mouth tighter. Had she expected to ask all the questions? Or did she think I was lying?

4

THE FIRST COUPLE OF WEEKS after school started, I could hardly sleep. It wasn't the fire or homework or any pressure. It was Anita. She was the first really good thing in my life for a long time.

I'd never been a stand-out kid. I tried to be upbeat around my mom and do what I was supposed to at school, but inside, I was pretty gray. My parents didn't push me to get good grades or take special lessons. I just rolled along doing whatever came up—bikes, sports, messing around with girls. When I thought about my life at all, I figured I'd follow the pattern: go to college, get a job, get married, have kids of my own, and my folks would be grandparents. Simple, straightforward. And then one evening in our kitchen Dad told me and Mom he'd met someone else and he was moving to Seattle. You meet someone new and then you leave your family? Is that how it works?

I hadn't seen that coming. I mean, I wasn't looking for it; Mom and Dad didn't do things like fight. I went to my room and trashed it; broke everything my dad had ever given me, even scissored up my baseball glove. My folks didn't try to stop me. Anyway, Dad left us. Gone by the end of the week.

I stopped caring what I did, stopped caring what I ate, got kind of hollow. Wib kept saying I seemed different, and Mom put me in therapy with a friend of hers for a month or so, but I didn't talk much. What was there to say? The marriage was just a piece of paper. The family was just a living arrangement. Dad was just a drifter looking for the best deal, passing through.

A couple of years later, another grenade. Dad and his new woman were killed in a car accident. Killed while I was hating him and wanting him dead. When Mom told me, I ran for my room but I didn't trash anything. I started crying and had trouble stopping.

Later Mom said I didn't speak for a couple of weeks. I don't remember that part. At the time, I was in junior high, ninth grade. I started taking choir because I liked sitting there listening to the music. I started doing sports so I wouldn't have to go to an empty house and wait for Mom to come home from work.

Wibby and Crane were neighborhood guys I'd known for years and walked home with from junior high. Sophomore year we all went downtown to Billings Senior High. In the middle of tenth grade Wib branched out and began to do a lot of hunting with his grandfather and some regular car mechanic work with his two uncles. I saw him less often after that.

Around that time Crane got heavy into sports—not football,

because he was tall and lean and easily injured, but he was first-string forward on the basketball team because of his three-pointer accuracy, and he was our fastest distance guy in cross and track. Long face, long legs, buzz-cut hair, he reminded me of photos I'd seen of the great high school miler Jim Ryun. Good-looking, funny, up for anything, he also got heavy into girls. He had the best music collection of anyone I knew, maybe a thousand CDs, and a dynamite sound system. Plus, his mom was a surgeon and he had access to her medicine cabinet. Always something to do at Crane's house.

By the end of sophomore year I'd started hanging out with a larger group of guys and girls on the weekends. I was pretty much back. Not really empty anymore. More like a bag of foam pellets, I could conform to whatever shape fit the moment.

Spring quarter, I'd started running track, and about that time I got to know Anita better, actually got pretty close on a choir trip. Last summer I found a part-time job stacking couches and other big items in a furniture warehouse. So gradually foam was getting exchanged for flesh. And then the Anita camping trip. I lay awake at night replaying our touching.

5

"YOU KNOW A GUY named Durmond Williams?" Childress, out of the blue.

"Durmie. Yeah—yes."

"Did you ever get angry with him? Hurt him?"

"Hurt him? I'm the one that got him to the emergency room. Check your records."

"Do you know who hurt him?"

"The nurse said he hurt himself. But I know who he was afraid of. Who he thought was after him."

Kosich was occupied picking lint off his slacks. "Why was somebody after him?" he asked, continuing to stand.

"Because Durmie was everywhere. He doesn't do the street corner sign thing like some of the homeless. He's all over town hustling, collecting stuff to sell. He sees a lot. People dealing, for example."

I'D RUN INTO DURMIE the first day of school, before things got so bad. I was just coming out of the locker room after practice, going to my car. He was sifting trash from the school outdoor garbage bins, collecting aluminum cans and glass he could recycle for money. I'd gotten to know him earlier in the summer. From time to time he came around the Dumpsters at the furniture warehouse, rummaging for damaged but still usable goods he could hawk or trade. I knew he'd been to our state mental hospital at Warm Springs several times because that was nearly the first thing he told me.

"Jeez," he had said, full of energy and enthusiasm, practically spitting as he talked, "I pretty much keep the ol' Springs going. They need me there! The staff is always forgetting stuff they got to do for us patients and I'm like the candy guy."

"Candy guy?"

"Yeah, yeah. I know how to bust through the red tape, get things done."

"Can-do guy?"

"Yeah."

"Why do you go there in the first place?" I had asked.

"Ah, sometimes I get too messed up. Been happening all my life . . . I can't explain it."

At one level he was a very simple guy, thin, wiry, probably in his late thirties. I don't think he could read or do any math except when it came to money. At another level he was very streetwise, very savvy. With his hustles he could make enough cash to keep himself in fast food. I thought he stayed overnights in some flop by the railroad tracks.

He yelled when he saw me walking toward him in the parking lot. "Got an extra can in your car?"

He wore a faded T-shirt over grubby jeans, torn canvas sneaks. As usual, he had on his Dodgers cap that rain had transformed into a wrinkled wad with a curved bill that he was constantly reshaping.

"Hey, Durm, how you doing?"

He was looking back and forth from the bins to me like he was trying to decide whether to put back the paper garbage he had pulled out onto the ground.

"Hey, I'm good. I'm good. You know me, always working . . . Hey, you want to give me a hand with this stuff? Somebody made a big mess here and I'm trying to clean it up."

Durmie said that with an absolutely straight face, as if his saying it made it so. I truly don't think he could imagine that someone else might see through the deception.

"Okay," I said, gearing up for another trip to Durmie's world.

"Hey," he said, leaning on the receptacle, watching me pick up the garbage, "how's your girl?"

"Hey yourself, brother," I said, putting another handful of trash in the can. "I'm helping you, remember? Bend your knees and get this stuff with me or I'm cutting myself in on your profit."

"Yeah, yeah. I was just resting a sec. I got a bad back, ya know. An' I got a bad liver and knees and my feet are all screwed-up. I probably got to get a surgical. I got coughing and my eyes get blurry—"

"Hey," I interrupted him. "Anita? You mean how's Anita?"

"Yeah. She got any tattoos yet? You don't got to tell me. She ask about me? She likes me, ya know."

I had introduced them. Anita and I had run into Durm two or three times around town when we were shopping and he was scrounging.

"She's good, man," I said, "and yeah, she asks about you time to time."

"For real?" Durmie lifted his cap for a sec and combed his hair with his fingers.

I didn't think he knew he was doing it.

"Yeah, for real. But, hey, she's my girlfriend, not yours."

Durm screwed his cap back on. "Yeah, yeah, I know. Just tell her I'm thinking about her."

I looked at him.

"In a good way, Teach. In a good way!"

He sometimes called me Teach. I never found out why, and it was true that Anita thought Durmie was sweet, fun, and I know she admired him for his grit.

"Durm," I said, nodding to the pile of garbage at his feet.

"Oh . . . yeah. Hey, I tell you I got some stomach trouble or something? Hurts when I bend over." He watched to see whether I would suggest that he not bend over and finish picking the stuff up.

I didn't.

"Yeah," he said, "well, okay." He leaned down and got the last of the garbage and lifted it into the can.

•   •   •

THE INTERROGATION OF GABRIEL JAMES

"WHO DO YOU THINK WAS AFTER HIM?" Kosich asked.

"The twins. Jules and Judd."

"Because he'd seen them selling?"

I nodded. "I think so."

"The twins?" he asked, pointing at the lump on my head.

6

OKAY, I want to hear more about what happened to him and Two Bull, but how did Raelene Ray come into the picture?" Childress again.

"It's complicated."

"Want a cup of coffee?" Childress looked to me, then to Kosich.

Kosich shook his head, yawned.

I did want one but I said no. Didn't want to seem like the weakest one.

Childress shrugged, raised her eyebrows.

"First, Anita broke up with me," I said.

SOMETIME DURING THE WEEK after the Laurel meet I'd driven home from practice thinking seriously about my running. I'd kept pace with a sophomore kid named Shugaart and a couple of guys from Laurel. I'd finished but hadn't placed. Once again hadn't scored. Mindless, really. Didn't want to be last. Kind of a reptilian instinct . . . the last get eaten. I hadn't pushed harder than I felt like going, never thought much about passing anybody. I had just rolled along enjoying the rhythm of the pace, the sun, the other guys around me doing the same thing. So, the questions remained. Would I help the team this year, or was I going to amble along doing my thing?

And what exactly was my thing? What would happen if I tried harder? What if I didn't have it in me? What if I was lazy? What if I really was pretty much at my peak? Or, what if I was better than I thought? Should I start pushing a little to see how it felt: my stride, the way I moved my arms, whether I could increase my pace but stay relaxed?

I had an ugly vision when I pulled into my driveway. What if I was in a car wreck and could never run again? Or worse. Could never walk. Would I be sorry I hadn't done more with my body while I could? I turned the car off, closed my eyes, and sat for a minute. Based on my history of ambition, would I shut down and fade away? Anyway, that had been on my mind. When I walked in I could hear grease popping. Could smell Mom frying hamburg with onions and chili for tacos.

"Anita called here looking for you," Mom said, glancing up from stirring. "She sounded upset but didn't say what it was about. Said to call her."

"Mind if I do that before dinner?" I asked, throwing my book bag on the couch and heading for the landline in the back hall where I could get some privacy.

Anita picked up after one ring. Her voice sounded raw.

"My folks found out, Gabe."

"What?" I thought maybe I hadn't heard her right.

She hiccuped. "Our neighbor my dad works with saw us in the café in Red Lodge. Mom said the man was talking with Dad today at lunch and he mentioned that he had run into us a while ago. He asked Dad if the family had taken a little mountain vacation before school started." She coughed, clearing her throat. "Dad was waiting for me when I got back from school today. He's ballistic. Mom understands, I think, but she's real disappointed."

I wasn't sure what to say.

"They know I lied and they found out about the birth control." She started crying and stopped talking for a minute. "I love you, Gabe. I—"

There was a loud bang like somebody hit her cell against something. The call cut out. I kept holding my phone. After a bit I clicked off.

I thought maybe I should go out to the kitchen and eat, but I just stood there. What if Mom asked me a question? What would I say? The idea of food repelled me.

My phone rang again.

"Dad hung up on—"

I could hear a struggle. She yelled, "Get away from me!" It sounded like the phone dropped and banged on the floor. I heard her mother's voice saying she'd handle this, and then there was an argument with several people yelling and talking at once. And then it was quiet.

Her mom's voice said, "Go ahead."

I could hear the phone being picked up.

"Gabe?"

Anita sounded horrible.

"Gabe?"

"Yeah."

"I can't do this," she said. "Somebody's gonna get hurt and I know it's my fault."

"Uh, should I come over?"

"No! God, no! They really don't want to see you. Maybe not ever. They told me to tell you not to come here again. Dad says you're no longer welcome in our house. I can't go out with you anymore."

At that moment all I could think about was resting my cheek against her hair, the scent of her shampoo. That neighbor saw us! How unlucky was that? I kept looking for a way to make this right.

"Anita, I love you, too!" *Did I?* "I'm so sorry. I'm . . . I never meant for this to happen. Let's just cool off for a couple—"

She broke in on me. "It's way past that, Gabe. You don't know how Dad is about something like this. He's out of control. It's too much. It's way too much."

"Anita, I—"

She cut me off again. "No! You've got to understand. I can't see you anymore. I can't. I really can't." She was crying again.

I could barely hear her mother's voice saying something to her.

"Gabe, I have to hang up now. Don't call me. Forget about me. We're done. We're really done."

I was scrambling for a foothold. "Anita, wait! Can I see you at school tomorrow?"

She was trying to get her breath.

"Gabe, remember my brothers? Remember they go there, too. Give it up. I don't want to lose my family. I can't see you anymore. Anymore, period." She hung up.

I sat on the straight-backed chair in the hall, unable to accept that we were over. No more messing around on choir trips. Her brother Duardo was in choir with us. No more weekend parties. No hanging around with her on school nights talking about whatever. She was the first girl I had ever been physically close to. I felt like someone had hit me. My neck ached, around the back like a crick. I might have yelled.

Mom was standing above me, holding a tortilla. "What's wrong?"

I turned to look at her. My mouth was open but I couldn't find any words. I looked away.

"That bad, huh? Well, I'm sorry. She seemed like a real nice girl."

I still didn't have anything to say.

"Dinner's getting cold," Mom said. "Come on in and have a bite, and then I'll clean up tonight and you can be alone or whatever you need. If you want to talk, we can talk before bed." She turned around and walked through the hall into the dining room and across the linoleum to the kitchen table. I heard her chair scrape as she sat down.

I couldn't think of anything else to do. My body went in. I gave eating a shot, but the food stuck in my mouth and I quit.

I was off somewhere else, wishing I hadn't talked Anita into that camping trip. Wishing I could remember every second of the last time we were together: the movie, whispering and kissing and sneaking touches no one else could see . . . when we had all the time in the world.

7

"SO CHAVEZ BROKE UP with you and you started on Raelene Ray?" Childress asked.

"No. That was a while later. Three or four weeks. Some other stuff happened before I got into it with Raelene."

"The attacks against Danny Two Bull?"

"Yeah, and things over at the Center."

"Start with Two Bull," Childress said. "Did you witness any of the attacks?"

"In a way, we all did." I wished there was at least a clock in the room, to distract my attention from what I was going to be saying. "The whole school knew about the red paint, the 'Shoot Crows' graffiti on the trophy case the Monday after the first time he won."

She waited.

"Did you know somebody nailed him with a slingshot?" I asked. "At the Missoula meet? He stopped and picked up the ball bearing and still came in first."

Childress shook her head, looked to Kosich. "You guys hear about that?"

Kosich shook his head once.

It felt good to know something they didn't. "And the thing about the rotten dog in his locker, and the fire on the Plenty Waters' porch?"

Childress nodded.

"Well, it all just made Danny madder. Harder. More determined."

"Anybody know who was doing it?" Kosich asked.

"Not then. Not till the Manifesto."

"How about at the Center?"

"Mom had said it seemed like the street people were getting more stirred up than usual. More hospitalizations. I decided to ask Durmie what was going on."

"You always call Williams Durmie?" Kosich asked, looking at the wall.

"Everyone does," I said.

I'D FOUND DURMIE AT THE CENTER. Buchanan Community Center was an old two-story brown brick building, a converted school, on Billings's south side. It sat on a corner of State Avenue and covered half a block in the area of town where unemployment was the norm, where the poor could find affordable housing, and where the homeless congregated. The place served a free hot lunch, and most days, after the meal, Durm would spend a couple of hours at the outdoor ball courts. He was ready to play any game, had every angle covered, took every edge, and thought nothing of bending rules to his advantage.

As I parked, two homeless guys, Bike Man and Lucius, were arguing by the front door. They stalked away from each other before I got there.

Over on the courts, Durmie was shooting baskets. Nearer, I could see he was practicing from the Around-the-World marks. It dawned on me that he probably bet neighborhood kids on games and played for money. He was concentrating and didn't see me until I was right beside him.

"Hey, Durm," I said, leaving him room to shoot. "What's down?"

"Hey, Teach, gimme a sec. I gotta hit five in a row an' I'm on three." He scrunched up his mouth to show how hard he was concentrating and made a Stations of the Cross maneuver with his left hand while continuing to dribble with his right, then sank the next two shots.

He spoke to me without taking his eyes off the basket. "Half-buck says I can make it six in a row. Whadaya say?"

I noticed him subtly edging closer to the basket. Still, I thought the bet would make him nervous and that he'd probably miss.

"You got fifty cents, you're on, Durm. You're good but you're no Jordan."

"It's a bet?" he said.

"Square deal," I said.

"Gotcha," he said, and calmly walked up and shot it in from one foot away.

"Hey!" I complained. "That's cheating."

"No way," he said, walking back to me with his hand out. "Nobody said from where. I just said six in a row." He was smiling to beat the band.

I reached in my pocket. No change.

He could see that. "Just give me a buck," he said. "I'll give ya the change later today."

"You said you had the fifty cents to pay if you lost," I countered.

"Aw, Teach," he said, shaking his head sadly. "I didn't need no fifty cents 'cause I wasn't gonna lose. Cough it up and I get ya back before you leave."

I knew I wouldn't see the change again, but he needed it more than I did. Before I handed it over, I asked my question again.

"So, tell me what's been happening around here lately and then Mr. Washington's yours. How come Lucius and Bike Man were arguing? I thought they were buds."

He rolled his eyes and shook his head in mock disgust. "Oh man, you don't want to know. You seriously don't. People getting wicked, fightin'. It's a crying shame . . . Double or nothing if I hit another shot from the free-throw line?"

I laughed. "You're way too slick for me. Just tell me what's going on."

He walked over to the shade by the wall and sat on a brick planter box.

"Okay," he said, "this is fresh dope."

I sat beside him and looked out over the playground so

39

if anybody was interested it would seem like we were just resting.

"We got some bad shit goin' down. 'Scuse my French, but people dissing each other, stealing, buying stuff they shouldn't ought."

"Who?" I asked him.

"Ah heck, Teach, I ain't no stoolie. You got eyes."

I guessed he meant Bike Man and Lucius, but who was buying? And what? Benzos? Meth?

"We got punks hanging around, messing with people, shouldn't even be here."

"What do you mean?" I asked him, leaning closer. "Who's hanging around? Bangers? Dealers?" Getting a report from Durmie was like getting a riddle without clues.

"Aw, they don't need hots and they don't need cots, ya know what I mean. An' hitting on people."

"Preying on women? Selling? Threatening people?" I asked, trying to get a picture. Mom would want to know.

"Players. Dudes. Just kids, really. Messin' with us," he repeated, exasperated. "Hell, I got no bizness talking this stuff. People got to tell you the selfsame." He looked away, past the playground out to the street. "Tell you this," he said. "You see two blondies, big yellow car? You cover up. But you didn't hear nothin' from me." He screwed his cap on tighter. "It's a shame, Teach. I'm getting bad, feeling bad, not even sleeping. I could hurt my own self, this keeps up. That's all I gotta say. Hurt or get hurt, you watch."

I was feeling a little exasperated myself. "Hey, we got weird

THE INTERROGATION OF GABRIEL JAMES

stuff going on at school, too, but nobody knows anything about it . . . or, nobody'll say anything. Tell me what you got and I'll tell somebody . . . or do something about it."

He snatched my dollar. "Hell no, Teach. It's getting to be every man for hisself. You check around. You'll see."

He tucked the basketball under his arm and walked away.

"WAS HE ALWAYS SO cryptic?" Childress was rubbing her forehead, perplexed. Kosich didn't appear to be listening.

"He was always kind of paranoid. He almost had his own language, very vague, so you couldn't hold something he said against him. It got worse when he was nervous."

"Worse?"

"More scared, more pessimistic."

"Did he ever spell it out? Name names, give you something we could use?" Childress asked.

"Blonds, big yellow car. Nothing more than that. He didn't want to admit it, but he was really scared. The next time I saw him was when I got him to the hospital after he tried to kill himself."

IN THE WEEKS THAT FOLLOWED, Mom had kept checking in at dinner, asking me whether I'd learned any more about the fire or the pets or the attacks on Danny, and I hadn't. Finally, maybe the Saturday after the Kalispell meet, I saw Bike Man wheeling up toward Pioneer Park and I waved him down.

"Bike, give me a sec."

He quit pedaling, coasted to a stop, but stayed on his rusty three-speed. He didn't look at me. Everybody but Lucius seemed to make him nervous.

"My mom's been asking me what's got people bothered at the Center and I don't know. Can you tell me what's going on?" I tried to say this like I was just a kid doing a good deed. Not nosy or anything, just helpful.

He didn't buy it. "Nothing. I got to go."

"Really? You don't usually argue with Lucius like you did the other day I was over at the Center."

He put his foot back on the pedal.

"And hey, I'm worried about Durmie. What do you think's happening with him?"

"Ask him."

"I don't know where he lives."

He pushed off leaving me with two words, "Coulter House."

Coulter House was an old three- or four-story brick hotel off 1st Avenue South. Since Durm hadn't been at the Center when I drove by earlier, I decided to try the hotel. Maybe he'd be more comfortable talking in his own digs. Maybe he'd tell me what he knew. I parked in front of a pawnshop and walked past a couple of vacant storefronts to the doorway under a faded sign with broken neon tubes.

Inside what once was a lobby were those old-fashioned white octagonal floor tiles, a bunch of them loose and all of them gritty. There was a front desk but no one behind it. A sign on the elevator said US STAIRS. Didn't seem to be any rooms on the ground floor. Most of the space was taken up by old washing machines and dryers with the coin receptacles pried out. These were pushed up against the back wall.

The stairs on the side of the lobby were carpeted but they shouldn't have been. Walking up, the stains were at eye level. Motor oil? Syrup? Blood? My stomach churned. At the top of the first flight a thin guy was standing in my way, smoking a cigarette. Stained navy pants, dirty Cal sweatshirt.

"Got change?" His eyes were yellow and he needed a shave.

"This a toll?" I asked him.

"Suit yourself," he said.

"I'm trying to help a buddy of mine," I said. "He lives here and he's a little shorter than me, pretty skinny, wears a beat-up Dodgers cap all the time."

He sized me up. I had several pounds on him and I was in pretty good shape. I could hear the rasp of his breathing.

"Probably could use a couple of bucks," he said.

"Him, or you?" I asked.

"Save you some time," he said.

I thought I had two singles in my wallet.

"Two, you take me right to his room."

He nodded.

"Let's do it," I said.

He led me up one more flight of stairs and past an open door where five or six guys were passing a clear pint bottle and playing cards. He pointed to a door at the end of the hall and held out his hand.

I walked past him and knocked on the door he'd indicated. It swung open, the jamb long since splintered, probably from somebody's kick. I could see Durmie on a single bed in the corner of the room. The place smelled like farts and spoiled food. I could sense the guy behind me. I faced him, gave him the money, and he walked away without another word.

I left the door open so I wouldn't gag. Durmie's eyes were closed. He looked like he hadn't been up for a couple of days. His hair was greasy and matted and he smelled awful. I shook his shoulder. He moaned. I said his name and shook him again, lightly. That's when I noticed the blood soaking the sleeve of his shirt nearest the wall.

"Durmie! Goddamn it!" I reached to my side and realized as usual I'd forgotten my cell in my car. Did Durm have a phone in his room? Right. I wasn't even sure this dump had electricity. I beat it down the stairs, raced outside, and nearly ran over a water company guy with a phone on his tool belt. He called it in and Durmie was in Deaconess Hospital within an hour.

8

OKAY. I NEED SOME COFFEE. YOU GUYS WANT SOME?"

I said I'd take a water.

Childress picked up her hat and stood. "They got a machine here somewhere, right?" she asked Kosich.

He shrugged. "Should have done this at the department," he said.

Kosich was a lump. I noticed when he shrugged, when he lifted his shoulders, his short neck disappeared, but his stomach stayed bigger than his chest or butt. What kind of cop was he? I couldn't imagine him chasing somebody. He was around the same age my dad would have been, but Dad had kept himself in shape.

I got to my feet and leaned over the table to do a half push-up and get my circulation going. The recorder was still on. Did Childress forget?

"Your mother have anything to do with this Ray thing?" Kosich asked.

That question ambushed me and made me uneasy. *Leave*

my mom out of this. "I told her about Raelene's situation but I didn't use the name, so really she didn't know anything about the Ray family."

"Huh," he said.

He didn't believe me?

"You know Crane was using?" he asked.

That also surprised me. I'd keep my guard up with this guy. I sat while I thought about the answer. "Uh, everybody uses something," I said.

"You're saying your teammates and the football players?"

"No. No. I mean once in a while. For fun. Most people."

"You take them, too?" he asked, turning to face me for the first time in the conversation.

The door opened and Childress came in with a Styrofoam cup in each hand and a bottle of water under her arm. She handed a cup to Kosich, sat, removed her hat, and pulled two candy bars out of her shirt pocket. "Breakfast?" she said, setting the water in front of me.

Kosich concentrated on sipping his coffee without burning his mouth.

I could feel my heart working.

"So somebody or -bodies were harassing Two Bull," Childress said, pushing some loose hair behind her ear and resting her hands on the table again.

"Beyond harassment," I said.

"Right. And somebody targeted the Center or at least the street folks and was causing trouble . . . and how does Raelene fit into this?"

"I don't think she actually 'fit' into it at all. She was near it. Just proximity."

Childress looked at Kosich. "Proximity," she said, but he didn't turn around.

Was she making fun of me? I went on anyway. "Raelene was in some of my classes. Wib told me she liked me."

"Wib your man Friday?" Kosich asked, sarcastic, like it was an insult.

"Not really. He . . . he doesn't really go out with girls himself. He's kind of a . . . a watcher. Sits in the back. Takes in the scene. Prompter-in-the-school-play type of guy. A manager, not a player, but always involved. There, but to the side."

"So he told you and what did you do?"

"Tried to check it out."

"Was it true?"

"Seemed to be."

ANITA AND I never spoke anymore. Cross-country league meets were in full swing and Danny had won regularly both at home and away. His times were starting to make headlines: "Two Bull Turns Up Heat in Helena." "Billings Runner Trips Great Falls." This in spite of the crap that was happening.

I had been planning to talk Wib into fishing the Stillwater with me on Sunday, but he derailed that when he told me about Raelene. There were several reasons I wasn't interested in his news. First off, I was busy rummaging in my locker after school, trying to locate my homework. Second, several times since Anita and I had broken up he had brought me news of someone's affection. None of them had worked out.

Third, Raelene was the girl who sat across from me in English, the shy, tidy girl who didn't seem to socialize, didn't seem to have either girl buddies or boyfriends. I brushed Wib off and didn't give it another thought until I saw her the following morning in geometry. She usually sat in the front corner of that class and I noticed that she tracked me with her eyes as I walked to my seat. Wib, who sought to arrive first in every class, was already seated in back and gave me a nod toward her when I waved a good morning to him.

I became interested in the idea at that moment, I think, because the whole thing seemed so unlikely. I wasn't a particularly popular kid. Sure, I did cross-country and track. I got decent grades and sang in the choir. No big deal. I wasn't flirting with her that I could recall. I mean, when I saw her I nodded pleasantly, usually, and that was it.

So, why me? I couldn't remember that we had ever really spoken. In English, across the aisle from each other, we didn't even have to pass each other papers. We didn't eat lunch at the same tables, she wasn't in the choir, she didn't go to meets or school games or dances. What would explain her interest? I was nice enough. Didn't think I was too cool or too tough, wasn't too handsome or too ugly, too rich or too poor. Maybe I seemed like a safe crush, maybe she liked my voice, or maybe Wibby was full of beans. I should have left it there, but I didn't.

I paid just enough attention to our geometry teacher to

understand how to do the class homework problems, and the rest of the time I watched Raelene. By the end of the period I was surprised. Her face was animated while she focused on understanding the math concepts. Obvious intelligence at work. She had always seemed ordinary to me. Her hair, I now noticed, was clean and shiny, hanging just past her neck, simply cut, not styled in any way. Her clothes reinforced that image: ironed white blouse, blue-green plaid skirt, and basic black flats. No ribbons or jewelry. No flash of any kind. In general, she was plain. Until you really looked, and then she was kind of pretty.

In a bright, no-nonsense way, she reminded me of my mom. I smiled as the thought "kindred spirits" came to mind, and I realized I didn't actually know a thing about her. My next thought was that I wasn't really interested. Wasn't interested in a new girlfriend. Was still getting over Anita. Was busy doing other things. The bell rang and brought me to my senses. Who was I kidding? But how did I know she really liked me? When Crane and Victor and I went out in the country drinking, Wibby would join us as the sober driver. What the hell did he know?

At lunch I walked outside the cafeteria around the cement patio area. Gumming my way through Mom's homemade peanut butter sandwich, I gave the matter some thought.

How do you know when someone likes you? They smile when they see you. You find them looking when you glance at them. They let you stand too close without moving away immediately. Maybe those things. But there's something unspoken,

49

something very subtle sometimes. Raelene had noticed me enter geometry class and looked at me as I walked to my seat. There seemed to be . . . what? Some kind of tiny electric current moving between us? A start maybe, so now I'd pay more attention.

I went over what I knew for sure about her. She was a junior. She was quiet. She seemed bright. She looked like the kind of girl who would work in the school office. She hadn't been in my junior high so she might have moved here in the last couple of years. In other words, next to nothing. After the bell rang, I asked Wibby how he heard she liked me, and what he knew about her.

"I can just see it. She's got the hots for you," he said, giving me a know-it-all smile.

I didn't comprehend Raelene from Adam, but I knew "the hots" was an exaggeration.

"I saw somebody driving her home from school last week out Rimrock Road, so she might live out west of town by the country club or out by Dell," Wib added.

Dell. That might explain the plain look and clothing. Years ago Dell had been a small settlement or some kind of religious community that was now just empty two-story wood houses and a derelict gas station/store, abandoned for all practical purposes. It was five or ten miles out on a narrow paved road where some of us went to drink beer or hike around looking for arrowheads in the summer.

"What kind of car?"

"A black Taurus."

"Decked out?"

"Nope. Cheap. Old. Crummy."

That sounded a lot more like Dell than the country club.

"Know anything else about her?"

"I've seen her talking sometimes with Emily Harper. Tall brown-haired girl that played the old lady in last spring's musical? Other than that, she usually eats in the cafeteria . . . and, uh, I think her mom must be real strict, or something."

"Why?"

"Because I sit right behind her, you know, they make us do first period alphabetically for roll call."

"Yeah?"

"Well, she *never* wears any lipstick or face stuff, and every day her outfit is different but the same, you know what I mean?"

"White shirt, dark skirt, black shoes?"

"Yeah, that's it."

AT THE NEXT CLASS BREAK I dropped by the office and asked Mrs. Spengle, an old neighbor who had recently become a clerk in the dean's office, where Raelene Ray lived.

"Now, why would you want to know," she said. She tilted her head and smiled at me with I-see-what-you're-up-to eyes.

"Come on, Mrs. Spengle," I said, shining her on. "A buddy of mine likes her."

She remained suspicious.

When she turned to answer the phone, Carrie, a student office volunteer and my fourth-grade girlfriend, came up to me.

"Is it Willoughby?" she whispered. "Willoughby has a heartthrob?"

"Working on it. You know Wib. He sits near her in a couple of classes and he's too shy to ask. Can you help him?"

She slipped me the address in less than a minute. Seventy thousand something Rapelje Road, out past the country club where the road to Dell turned off Rimrock Road. Dell it was.

Later that day, in English, I loafed around right by the door and smiled at Raelene when she walked past me into class. She glanced at my face and smiled right back, but she never broke stride on her way to her seat.

That night, after cross, I drove the road to Dell. Out past the city limits there were some fancy newer cedar-log and ranch-style houses with manicured lawns and elegant pastures. Farther out, sagebrush prairie, most of it fenced by local ranchers who ran cattle. In the quarter moonlight I could see distant windmills and occasional livestock water tanks. Bulletholed mailboxes here and there along the highway postmarked the older places at the end of dirt roads.

Dell turned out to be just like I had remembered it. Weathered, boarded-up houses, gray with the barest scratches of paint remaining. Out-of-business gas station, windows long ago shot out. One mercury vapor lamp near the middle of the five or six buildings. No cars, no interior lights, no dogs, nothing except a worn FOR SALE sign on a corner post.

The next day, Friday, I got to geometry early, took up a position just inside class, and I did it. Spoke to her. Said her name. Said hello.

She started at the sound of my voice, actually took a half step to the side on her way through the door, and she blushed, smiled the rest of the way to her seat.

Wib was right, she does like me. I grinned all the way to mine.

That afternoon we ran against Skyview and West High. Danny was first, with their guy Banks edging Crane and their guy Kerwin edging Sparks. Shugaart got fifth. I'd actually placed against Helena and Great Falls, but this time I was missing in action. I know I finished. That's about it.

OVER THE WEEKEND I asked friends for more info about Raelene. Crane knew who she was and said once in a while he'd seen her talking with Emily in the halls or at lunch. He confirmed that she seemed nice enough, but she was totally out of the social scene. Too mature? College boyfriend? Didn't seem like it. I was pretty sure she wasn't sophisticated like that. Too religious? Remnant of that spiritual community? Her dad was a preacher? Her mom's a fundamental evangelical something or other?

I was stumped. No one else I asked, including Sparks and Shugaart, knew anything really. Victor thought she transferred in as a sophomore from some place in California. Good grades. Quiet. No activities. I even called Emily about her, but I didn't know Emily very well and she wouldn't say a thing and didn't seem to welcome my questions. She was downright stiff, which surprised me since I thought that maybe Raelene would have talked to her about me and that she might be kind of glad to know that I was interested.

Monday, my faithful office snoop, Carrie, came through

with more details. Raelene had a brother. Carrie thought his name was Homer. Thought he was a sophomore or junior, apparently homeschooled, but he brought Raelene every morning and picked her up after classes. Occasionally he came into the office to collect individual math assignments from one of the algebra teachers. When I asked around, the few who had seen him agreed. Quiet, slim, short brown hair, jeans, didn't seem to have any close friends. Victor had met the kid once in the office and recognized the last name, Ray, because it's fairly unusual, but didn't know the kid's first name. Jeez, I thought when I heard that. This family's damn near invisible. Anyway, it was obvious. The only way to find out more about Raelene would be personal, up close. Get to know her, pure and simple.

Tuesday, I sat next to her at lunch. She turned quickly, startled, when I sat down. Then she looked back at her plate, blushing pretty strongly. I could understand. It was kind of a brazen move, since mostly guys sat with guys, girls with girls.

"Hi," I said, "I'm Gabe."

She said, "I know."

"I have some classes with you," I said.

She said, "I know."

I said, "I uh, run; I'm on the cross-country team."

She nodded.

I asked if she understood the theorems today in geometry. I said I thought they were pretty complicated.

She nodded.

I asked her if she would like part of a peanut butter sandwich.

She said, "No thanks, I've got to get going," and stood up, picked up her half-finished plate of macaroni and cheese and her milk, and left for the cleanup window.

I sat there for a while chewing my sandwich, and when a few minutes had passed, I looked around casually to see if anybody had noticed the brush-off. Everybody else was talking and eating. I thought about what had happened. She had blushed again. Why? Because she liked me, or because I embarrassed her? I ran her off. That much was clear. Well, I thought, getting up, at least she knew I was interested.

For the rest of the day and Wednesday I continued to be pretty sure she liked me. We talked a bit on the way to English, nothing deep, but pleasant and friendly. Thursday I asked her to go to the dance in the gym after the game on Friday. She turned me down flat. Not mean, but very firm. She said she couldn't date and we couldn't be like that and then she said maybe we shouldn't talk together anymore. Friday she didn't even look my way. Weird.

I thought maybe she was actually going out with somebody else and I hadn't discovered it. I asked Crane, who was going out with Genelle, the gossipy queen-bee cheerleader, to scope it out. He said she said nobody. I asked Diane in choir if Raelene was seeing someone in music or band. Nope.

I didn't have time to clear things up with Raelene after school on Friday because of the meet with Butte High—Danny won again and their team was real weak so I got fifth—no big deal—but that following Monday I stopped her at the beginning of lunch and asked her what was going on. She turned away from me and didn't say anything. Plus, Emily wouldn't talk to me in the hall the next time I saw her.

I was having trouble with the silent treatment, annoyed actually, because I felt certain that she liked me and I didn't think I'd done anything special to turn her off. I just plain didn't get it.

9

IS THAT when you started to stalk her?" Childress asked, looking at her hands.

I was up before I could stop myself. "Are you nuts? Who's telling you this? Is it the Guru? Raelene's dad? God, look at him. He's crazy!"

Childress didn't flinch, continued leaning back, easy in her chair. Kosich had picked his Styrofoam cup to pieces.

"I never stalked her," I said, sitting again.

"What would you call it?" Kosich pushed his chair farther from Childress's side of the table and sat down at an angle to me.

"I followed her. From school. I had to. I needed to understand why she was acting that way."

Kosich looked at me for the first time in a while.

I looked away. "I mean I didn't have to, but she liked me for a couple of weeks and then she froze up, and I hadn't done anything. Ask Emily. Nothing. I asked her out. That's all I did. And after that she started avoiding me."

"Emily," Childress said.

"Emily Harper. She was Raelene's only friend. At least the only one I could find."

"You were making a study of Raelene?" Childress had a way of asking these questions with absolutely no inflection in her voice, but the words themselves felt ominous. She and Kosich were so damned unreadable. Made my stomach growl.

"No. Do you want to understand or not?" I said. I had meant to sound irritated but it came out whiny.

She looked at her hat, pushed it an inch further from the table edge. Kosich seemed distant again, resting his chin on his palm, eyes closed.

"She, Raelene, said she liked me. You can check that out."

I watched as Childress made a check mark on a clean page of her pocket notepad. Meaningless, or a reminder to verify everything I was saying?

"Then after I invited her to the dance, she said she couldn't do things like that and began totally shutting me out. There couldn't be someone else. It didn't make sense."

"You were jealous and you started tailing her?" Childress asked.

She thinks I'm a sleaze. "Curious," I said, trying to keep my voice flat, "just curious."

"And?"

"And? I followed her. Exploring. To know her a little. I told you that. Her brother picked her up from school in a black Taurus and I tracked them in my car. After I found out where she lived, I . . . I left and came back later that night, a couple of hours after dinner. I mean, that might make me sound like a perv, but I was just heading out there to see what was going on. See if she was okay."

EVEN WITH THE HIGH CLOUDS, the moon illuminated the ranches and sagebrush hills like a scene on a Christmas card. I parked across from her dirt road facing my car east, hoping, if anybody wondered, that they would assume my car had broken down and I was walking back toward Billings. I hiked up the rutted single lane that the Ford had taken earlier. At the top of the short hill the road turned through a cattle guard. Twenty or thirty yards farther along the crest, the road divided at another fence, tire marks passing through an opened stock gate. The crest played out and the road angled along the north slope of the ridge on a gentle decline. About three hundred yards down, an old square two-story house bordered by a stand of cottonwood came into view.

I stopped still for what seemed like five minutes to see if I would be discovered and barked at by any dogs. Nope. That was surprising. Almost everyone I knew who lived in the country had at least one dog to warn them if unexpected company was coming and to keep critters out of the yard. While I waited I noticed a horrible smell coming from a gully to my left. A horse or a cow must have died. The odor slid away as I walked closer to the house. The Ford was parked by a porch on the far side.

When I reached the rough grass yard, I could hear bits of a news broadcast inside. I walked around to the front of the house, up to the porch steps, and stopped, looking at the closed front door. The porch was dark, but in the half-light I could see shapes to the right of the entrance. There, hanging on a nail or a clothes hook, was Raelene's blouse, her skirt, and, in a tidy pile on the porch floor, her black shoes and her underwear. I don't know how long I looked at that before I saw the other hook next to it, holding a boy's shirt and jeans and, beneath, a white T-shirt and jockey shorts folded on top of black oxfords.

I left then, because I couldn't make myself look in the windows.

"YOU DIDN'T LOOK IN," Childress clarified.

"No. It creeped me out. I left."

"Think I'm ready for more coffee," Kosich said, as he rose and walked to the door. "I'll bring a couple."

Childress was still looking at me.

I couldn't hold her eyes.

10

HOW DID HOMER RAY know Danny Two Bull? They have a run-in at school?"

"Homer . . . hard to believe that's his name," I said, thinking out loud. That would have cost him. Guys would tease the hell out of him. "And the Guru, their father, what's his name?"

"Sun Ray," Childress said.

I didn't know if she was serious. "Like sunshine?" I asked. No response.

I went on. "I don't think they met at school. Homer, I think, was homeschooled. By his dad. That must have been rank."

"So you left the Rays' house that night. But you came back. You couldn't leave it alone?" Kosich had returned.

I realized why he was pissing me off. While Childress seemed to withhold judgment most of the time or at least usually gave no particular indication how she felt, Kosich put a negative spin on things. Or was it his tone of voice? Something. He didn't like me. Or maybe he thought this whole interrogation was a big waste of breath like they should just arrest me and get on with it. Whatever the explanation, it seemed to me like his head was someplace else a lot of the time. Why was he here? Where had I seen him?

"I tried other ways to figure it out. I decided to get to know her friend Emily. She'd told me Raelene was very guarded about dating and things like her home life."

"Why didn't Emily go see what was going on?" he asked.

"I never got to know Emily that well. A, Emily has a boyfriend, a guy at college, so we talked together a few times but we weren't exactly close. I don't really understand her. And B, the whole thing with Raelene bothered Emily. She said she thought meddling in the situation, whatever it was, would make it worse. She didn't want to be involved."

"Any more involved."

"Yeah."

EMILY. Trying to get a line on Raelene, I'd gone to school early looking for Emily. She was in the college prep group and had classes at different times than I did because of some work-study arrangement that took her out of school a couple of days a week.

She was a terrific actress. She stole the show last year in the musical when she played an old woman. She was so good I actually believed they'd imported somebody's grandma. Physically she looked like she could be a runner, and she was tall enough to play forward on the girls' basketball team, but she didn't do either, at least not for the school. She usually wore her hair in a French roll or twist or whatever they called it. She was lean with a narrow face, and was she stoop-shouldered, or was that just something she did for the old-woman part? So, tallish, slenderish, light brown hair. That's as close as I could come, but I believed I'd know her when I saw her.

I couldn't find her before class started. I asked Genelle, and she said Tuesdays and Thursdays were Emily's intern workdays but that she usually got back to school in time for sixth-period study hall. Okay, I'd get out of choir early using cross as an excuse and wait for her at the study hall door.

As she walked out I said her name loud enough to get her attention. When she saw who it was, she frowned.

"Hey, please," I could hear the edge in my voice. "I really need to talk with you just for a minute."

She tried to sidestep me. I retreated but stayed in front of her.

"Emily, I haven't dissed you or Raelene. You don't need to act like this."

Her eyes blazed. "I don't talk about my friends," she said, "and you and I don't know each other, so we don't have anything to talk about!" She started walking past me.

"Something weird is going on at Raelene's place," I said as she got even with me.

She wheeled, scowling and breathing hard, and for a second I thought she was going to take a swing at me. In a few moments she settled down a little and said, "It's none of your business."

"What if she's caught up in something and that's why she acts so strange at school?"

"If this is some kind of dirty manipulation to go out with her when she doesn't want to, so help me god, Gabriel, I'll scratch your eyes out." Her hands were clenching and unclenching.

I didn't say anything.

"She doesn't need any more trouble in her life," Emily said, speaking softly but emphasizing the words very clearly.

"I'm totally sure that's true." I let that sit for a moment.

Emily was no longer trying to walk away.

"Do you know what goes on at her home?" I asked.

She took half a step closer to make our conversation a little more private. "No," she said. "Not really. She doesn't want me to visit."

"That's what I'm talking about. I thought maybe you knew something and were trying to help, or maybe you didn't know and would want to help her. I couldn't think of who else to go to . . . and that's all." I stopped and kept my eyes up and let her assess me, decide if I was lying.

We stood there. Until she said "Oh god!" and turned and practically ran down the hall. This time I didn't try to stop her. At least she had heard me. And it meant something to her. Maybe she would be willing to talk about it tomorrow. After she was gone, I realized Raelene must have talked about me, told her my name. I wondered if that was good or bad? And as I walked away I still wasn't sure exactly what her face looked like.

"SO THE HARPER GIRL didn't know anything substantial about the Ray compound," Childress said.

"Compound?"

"All those buildings are his," Childress said. "He has a hundred and sixty acres, including the home you went to and the ghost town buildings and barn on the other side of the ridge by the road."

"No, she didn't know anything about the home itself, but she did have more information about Raelene."

THE NEXT DAY AT LUNCH Emily handed me a note as she walked out of the cafeteria. It had her cell phone number and said to call. I couldn't remember whether a girl had given me a note before. In spite of the fact that I knew it was about serious business, I felt flattered. And even attracted.

I phoned her when I got home after cross and said I could come visit in a while before I started doing my homework. I rushed dinner, told Mom I didn't have time for the dishes, and drove to her place.

She lived in a cozy older neighborhood with tree-lined streets and two-story wood-frame houses. I parked under a canopy of limbs and, with most of the leaves on the ground now, I could see stars winking through the branches. The air was cool, and someone in the neighborhood was baking a cake or cookies. Mom never made cookies. She tended to incinerate anything that took over ten minutes to cook. She'd get busy reading and forget it was on the stove or in the oven.

Emily opened the door herself. It must have been the neighbors that were baking. Since I was attuned to smell at that point, I noticed that somebody in her family enjoyed scented candles, coconut or vanilla, and that they probably had a dog. When I looked at Emily she had a funny expression.

"Well," she said, "do we pass the nose test, or should we fumigate?"

I was embarrassed. "I was just sniffing for cookies. Walking from my car, I thought I smelled some."

"That's Mr. Fournier," she said, smiling. "He's always making pastries and sweets. He brings us samples all the time. It's a wonder I'm not a blimp."

We were still standing in her front hall. I took a moment to look at her. Her shoulders didn't really stoop but they were small, her wrists delicate. She had light brown eyes to match her hair and a clear, light tan complexion. Her nose was sharp and big for her face. Put together with high cheekbones it made her look serious and distinguished. Mom might have called her handsome, which I was never sure really applied to a girl.

"Do you want to talk here, or are you willing to venture a little farther inside?" she asked, teasing, her face softening with a half smile.

"Sorry," I said, "I just had never really looked at you before." That didn't sound right.

She cocked her head at me.

"I mean I only really ever knew you from the play and I was just studying how different you look when you're real."

"Well, Mr. James," she said, eyebrows arched, teasing again I hoped, "you certainly have a way with words. Let's talk in the kitchen."

We walked through the living room where her mom was sitting on the couch with her dad, watching some science thing on TV. Emily introduced me and they welcomed me and then turned back to their program. She and I sat at the dark wood table next to the breakfast bar.

"Want a soda or some water?" she asked.

I said no thanks.

She put her chin on her hands, settled in. Pursed her lips, getting serious. "Raelene," she said.

I told her that the idea of the Rays' home life gave me the creeps and made me wonder if her dad was a molester. I said I knew that in a lot of ways it was none of my business, but I also knew that, for a brief bit, Raelene had liked me and then she backed away before we could even try a date. She had shut down, like doing anything together was totally out of the question. Now, I didn't want to date anymore, but I was curious about her and I thought maybe she needed help.

I told Emily my mom was a social worker who said sometimes County Child Protective Services helped kids that were being harmed by their family situation. I paused to gauge her reaction.

She rubbed at an eyebrow, still giving me her full attention.

I went on. "I finally figured that you probably knew her better than anyone else. I didn't want to blow things up by making some kind of report on her family. I decided to take this to you and see what you thought. If you knew she was okay, I would just drop it."

I realized I had been leaning across the table closer to her as I talked. Was it her eyes that made me think she was almost beautiful?

She sat back and exhaled like she had been holding her breath.

"First of all," she said, "I don't have to tell you that Raelene is really really shy, and she's very backward and sheltered. I mean, she's book smart, you probably know that, too, but she doesn't read magazines or go to movies or dances. She definitely doesn't date. It's a compliment to you that she showed you any interest at all, but she would be way over her head going out. Her mom either died or left when Raelene was a baby and she's been raised by her dad. She says he's super strict."

Emily was absentmindedly twisting a strand of her hair. I wondered if talking about this stuff made her nervous like it did me.

"I don't think she has any real life experience, not even church," she said. "Her dad used to be some sort of maharishi or guru person and had a commune-type thing out around Dell. The commune came apart years ago and now it's just them, the Rays, out there by themselves. She says he's against organized religion and the government and just about everything else. That's why he continues raising her and her brother out in the country. She says he doesn't like or trust other people . . . In short, you're right. He's totally weird."

"Huh," I said. "So, does she need to be rescued?"

Emily bit her bottom lip. "Well, I don't think that's any of our business. I mean, she hasn't asked me for help, or even hinted that she would like help." Emily looked to the living room where we could now hear a phone ringing. "She seems a little afraid of her dad. I guess he doles out the punishment when she or her brother makes a mistake. But mostly I think she feels sorry for him. He's a shut-in. Doesn't have any friends. She and her brother are his whole world."

Her mom walked into the kitchen holding a cell phone. "It's Mark, for you, honey."

"Mark?" I asked.

"My boyfriend," she said. "He's in drama at the university in Missoula." She took the phone and got up. "I'll just be a couple of minutes," she said, looking like she was getting ready to go to another room.

"No problem," I said. "I have to take off anyway."

Her mom showed me to the door.

College boyfriend. That note passing didn't mean anything much at all.

11

THAT FRIDAY AFTERNOON we'd whacked Bozeman, came in one, two, four, and six. Six? Me. And I was close enough to Sparks and the fifth guy to hear them puffing. Their best runner was out with the flu and Danny's time was back to mid-sixteen, so the race wasn't exactly a sprint, but still. I did what I had been working on. Warmed up the right amount, picked the fastest stride I could live with, and let following Sparks carry me up the hill part. At the end, the last quarter, I actually had a bit of a kick. Totally surprised Shugaart. Left him in the dust.

After the football game that night, I ran into Emily at the dance. We said hi and she seemed comfortable with me so I asked her to dance to a couple of fast ones. We were still out there when the DJ put on a slow song. I really liked the way she melted in close while we moved around the floor. Her back was warm and she smelled fresh like soap and lilacs. At the end of the song I found myself wanting to hold her hand while we walked back to the bleachers.

I didn't.

We found an empty spot and sat down together.

"So, how long have you been going with the actor?"

"Mark?" she asked. "Since the play last year. If you saw it, he was the lead. But he doesn't really want to be an actor. Long term he wants to direct. He wants that kind of control."

"Is he fun?" I asked.

"Fun? . . . No, not really. He's pretty serious, but he's really bright and talented. And very ambitious. He told me a couple of days ago he wants to transfer to NYU. To their drama department. Closer to where the real action is, as far as he's concerned. I like him a lot but I don't think our relationship would last if he did that."

I wanted to sympathize with her, to say that would be a shame, but instead I was feeling kind of perked up. Go figure. I told her I enjoyed dancing with her and suggested maybe we could do it again in a couple of weeks at homecoming.

Wibby gave me a sloppy grin when I joined him. "Nice rebound," he said, shaking his head as if I were incorrigible.

Crane was on the gym floor dancing with Genelle. He looked out of it, really tired or even stoned.

Victor walked up to stand with us and smiled. "She's kind of something, isn't she?" he said, nodding toward Emily and her group.

LATER, shortly before everything blew up, I almost convinced Emily to date me. I'd gotten a phone call from her asking if I had time to come by her house again. Sure. Maybe she had some new information. Maybe she just wanted to see me.

She opened the door just before I knocked and we walked to the kitchen without speaking. Took our places at the dining table.

"Thanks for coming."

"Why aren't you somewhere doing something?" I asked.

"Well, that's one of the drawbacks of having an out-of-town boyfriend."

"I can see that."

"How come you're not doing anything?"

That was the day I'd found Durmie bleeding in his room. "I ran into a friend who came close to killing himself."

"From our school?"

"No, a street guy named Durmie. He's got serious problems but he's also funny and very gutsy. He's a survivor, collects cans, finds sellable trash, whatever it takes. He's been in and out of mental hospitals all his life and I think he got sideways to punks dealing stuff to his friends. Maybe he couldn't handle the bind of watching it continue or ratting people out. Anyway, I got him to the hospital and he's in I.C.U."

"I'm sorry."

"Yeah, it's a big mess and I'm glad you called because I was probably going to get in more trouble before the night's over."

Emily was studying me. Deciding something?

She put her hands out flat on the table and started talking. "I've been thinking about my friendship with Raelene since you told me about her home situation. Trying to remember all the things she ever said about it.

"Once, I offered to drive out and pick her up on a weekend

night. Go to a show or at least get a burger and cruise a little bit. She said she couldn't do anything like that. Said her dad wouldn't let her. I pushed, saying she was a junior in high school, and saying that her dad was way over-the-top strict, and that I thought she needed to have it out with him. She said it wouldn't do any good because he wasn't well. Plus, he was really opinionated and set in his ways. He wouldn't take her seriously. He wouldn't even discuss things like dating. Not an option. Said she had given up trying years ago. I said that must be pretty tough. She said, 'Yeah and my brother is even worse.' I said like how? She said to forget she even mentioned it, because there's nothing that can be done.

"She told me that when she was older she'd get away but for now she needed to take care of them. Both of them. From then on, she wouldn't talk about her family. When I'd ask, she'd say that she shouldn't have said anything and for me not to worry about her."

"What did she mean about her brother being worse? You think he's getting together with her?"

"I don't think so but I don't know. I didn't pick up anything."

KOSICH HAD STARTED FUMBLING with the notebooks on the interview table before I finished my sentence. Did they contain evidence about incest?

"Listen to this," he said, holding one open to a dog-eared page.

Childress reached across the table and covered the page with her hand.

Kosich closed the book and set it back on the stack. "So outside the house, when it's just the two of them, they don't act weird," he said, glancing toward the closed book. "Homer thinks his sister's pretty but says he doesn't mess with her."

"I think that's true," I said. "I mean I saw that, them in the car."

"Must have been a temptation," Kosich went on, "sixteen- or seventeen-year-old guy. Around his sister all the time while she's growing up. " He exhaled, not quite a sigh. "Apparently the dad didn't mess with her either, but the kid was worried something would happen to her one of these days. Said *one of us could hurt her*."

Childress picked up on that. "One of us? Him or his dad? Him or one of his other identities?"

"Not sure. The kid said he knew Sun Ray loved her, thought his dad had behaved okay up to now, but was getting crazier."

"Was the dad on psych meds?" Childress asked.

"Don't know. Never heard," Kosich said. "About him or Homer. The boy's a wacko but he was dealt a bad hand."

"He's a head case. Classic split personality," Childress said.

"Vernon Ray," Kosich said, changing the subject.

"The Guru? The father's original name?" Childress said.

"Yeah. I'm remembering now. He changed it to Sun Ray when he started the commune. Called it the Dell. God, he could talk! Like Martin Luther King. Rapped for hours, days, about Plato and our responsibility to live the Ideal. Answer any question. You never saw anything like it. Donations,

74

volunteers, folks just wanting to be around him. That barn? He called that the Planetorium. The commune was a huge deal for a while. You should have seen it."

Childress shot Kosich a look, reached over and turned off the recorder. "Time for a breather," she said.

Kosich turned his back on us but went on. "Took in the lost and loony," he said. "Wound up helping a bunch of people. That was before Buchanan Center opened. The Dell had this huge garden and sold produce to local restaurants. Built the buildings themselves. Had a good heart."

Childress looked restless. Put her Stetson on but didn't stand. Brushed something off her sleeve, began clicking her ballpoint. Was Kosich saying too much?

I was fascinated. Compound? Commune? I'd never heard about anything like it around here. I mean, you hear about crazy cults on the news but you never hear about them doing anything good. And Kosich. How did he know so much about that place? You wouldn't expect a cop to say things like that about a cult.

Kosich was facing the wall away from the mirror. Talking to it like we weren't even in the room. "After the classes on the weekends they'd have big parties. Had their own band. Got raided three or four times. At one of their parties, the wife-trading they used to do got somebody mad and the guy shot Ray. I think it was a guy. Paralyzed him for a while. He was in the infirmary here," he said, nodding toward the lockup clinic over on the other side of the parking lot. "They found all sorts of drugs when they searched the grounds, and since Ray was the owner they charged him. He did a stretch in Deer Lodge. At least a year hard time. Sun Ray. The ladies' man. Guru to con."

Kosich shook his head and stopped talking. "Did you know any of that?" he asked Childress.

"The history? No. All before I moved to Billings." She had caught her bottom lip in her teeth and was unscrewing her ballpoint like she was going to check the cartridge.

Kosich waited till she stopped fiddling and raised her eyes. He held her look for a moment before rejoining us at the table.

"Anyway," Childress said to me, "you were telling us about Emily." She flicked the recorder on again and put her hat down.

I thought something important had just happened between them but I wasn't sure what. "Why do you want to hear all this?" I asked. "Don't you know what happened? Are you going to arrest me for trespassing or accessory or something?"

"Everybody sees too many cop shows," Childress said, shaking her head. "Well, trespassing. That might fit if Ray wanted to press charges. Accessory, possible if you're lying. Obstruction? That fits. Depends on what the D.A. wants to do after he hears this," she nodded at the recorder.

Did Kosich glance at the mirror? I wasn't sure.

"Right now," Childress continued, "I'd say you're still in the category of material witness. We have a double homicide we have to explain to the powers that be and we need to get the whole story right and tight." She looked at me to see how this sat. "Okay?"

What could I say? I hadn't figured out in my own mind how much I was to blame.

12

"WHEN I WAS TALKING WITH EMILY, a little before the end,"
I said, "she told me Raelene's brother had made up a
name for himself."

"MDD?" Childress asked. "Hornet?"

"She said she couldn't remember. Just that it was something odd."

EMILY AND I had stayed quiet in her kitchen for a while. I remember trying to imagine what it would be like to grow up in
a house where I had to take off my school clothes at the front
door, and where my dad was a crazy ex-guru. First off, I would
be terminally embarrassed. Couldn't invite anybody home with
me. Probably couldn't have close friends. Wouldn't want anyone
to find out, ever. And seeing my sister naked all the time . . .
Was she really naked? Did they put on robes or something? Did
they have to undress or change clothes together? What would
that do? Wouldn't that begin to make her like my girlfriend or

even my wife? . . . Or would it just make me want to puke? And how would I feel about myself?

I must have cringed picturing it.

"This is too weird," Emily said, holding her arms like she was cold.

"You want to go out and get a Coke, a soda? Or something?" I checked her reaction, afraid she might laugh at me.

"Huh," she said. "That might be good. Get some fresh air. This Ray stuff makes me feel yuck."

"There's supposed to be a band at Ersatz," I mentioned.

Ersatz was a club for teenagers out west of downtown in the industrial section on King Avenue. The bar sold soda and coffee. You could score beer or drugs in the parking lot if you wanted to, but most kids I knew—Victor, Crane, Wib, the cross team—just went to hang out and dance on weekend nights when nothing special was happening. Anyway, going to Ersatz together was a pretty big escalation from going to the Burger Bin for a soda. I was thinking about dancing with her.

I looked at her again and she had her head cocked, eyes squinted, looking back at me.

"No, I'm not sure that would be a good idea . . ."

I stayed quiet, tamping down the disappointment.

"Wait," she said, thinking out loud. "It's not a date. It's friends. Friends trying to help another friend . . . Sure!" she said, breaking into a smile. "Or is that a rationalization?"

I couldn't find any words to answer her and just laughed. I was excited.

• • •

THERE MUST HAVE BEEN fifty kids hanging out around their cars and smoking in the parking lot between the teen club and the John Deere tractor warehouse next door. I paid the ten-buck cover and we waded through the wall-to-wall crowd toward the bandstand. Twenty feet in, we ran into Genelle and Crane coming out of the tangle of dancers.

"Well, well," Genelle raised her eyebrows. Her face was taking on one of those I-knew-this-would-happen expressions. "So, Emily, you're willing to risk your reputation being seen in public with this guy?"

I could see Crane smiling at me in the background, but I could feel Emily stiffening on my arm, stopping, subtly starting to back up.

"Hi," Emily was saying. "Oh, you know, we just . . . we had some schoolwork to do together and decided to get out of the house for a little exercise. Good band?"

She had my hand trapped under her elbow and was levering me into turning with her as she maneuvered back in the direction of the door. "I forgot my purse," she said over her shoulder. "See you in a minute." She gave them a half wave and we were again pushing our way through the crowd in the opposite direction to the entrance.

When we were outside she stopped at the first row of cars. Faced me.

"I can't do this," she said. "Genelle's going to broadcast around school that we're dating and Mark will catch wind of it and . . ." She looked away toward the Rims and the pine trees silhouetted against the sky.

"I don't know what I'm doing," she said, crossing her arms against the chill.

We stood by a dark Subaru that still had a little snow clinging to the windshield, as if the driver had come down from the mountains for tonight's dance. I was searching my mind for a compelling argument that would convince her to come back inside with me.

"Let's go," she said, wheeling around, moving toward my car. "I'll pay you back for the cover."

"Want to get some fries on the way home?" I asked, hoping to salvage some of the close feeling we had experienced earlier.

"No," she said without looking back.

I unlocked her door first. Walking around to my side, I noticed two blond guys standing by a light yellow Impala parked a row over on the edge of the lot. Two punks, big yellow car, just like Durmie had told me. I was still staring when Emily leaned over and popped the lock on my side.

CHILDRESS CLEARED HER THROAT. "So Emily winds up being peripheral to what happened."

"Mostly," I said, "but, like I'm telling you, we were together when I got a line on the blonds, the yellow car."

"Got a line." Kosich shook his head like I was disappointing him with my stupid TV language.

"After I saw them, I took Emily home, and found them again later that same night at Durmie's place."

• • •

WHEN I HAD RETURNED to the parking lot they were gone. I drove to the Center to see if I could find them. Nothing. And then, on a hunch, I drove to the Coulter House. The Chevy was parked across the street.

The lobby didn't stink as bad at night when it was colder. I climbed the stairs to Durmie's floor. The halls were empty and the doors to the other rooms were closed. When I got close to his door I could hear voices inside. I had a quick thought that maybe I should leave. Call the police.

I should have. But I guess I was mad, too. Without making a conscious decision, I kicked the door open. It didn't dawn on me until later that I could have been shot. Across the room, by the street-front window, a blond kid with a burr cut was sticking a knife into Durmie's threadbare red-white-and-blue basketball. He froze when he saw me. Another kid walked from the dark side of the room and came to face me. Blond spiked hair. Looked exactly like the kid with the knife. Twins probably, brothers for sure.

"You're in trouble," I said, measuring him for a punch.

The spike-haired kid charged me. I didn't even get my hands up and I was sailing back through the door into the wall across the hallway. The kid's shoulder went right into my stomach and all the air whooshed out of me as I slid to the floor.

The other one said, "Let's split," and I heard steps hustling out of the room and clomping down the hall. I raised my head and one of them kicked me and I folded.

By the time I came around, they were gone. It took me a

while to get my wind back. When I sat up, my neck was wet. Blood. Coming from my ear, probably from the kid's shoe. I stood and went in Durmie's room, looked out the window. Their car was gone. I still didn't know who they were. Remembering the way their steps sounded, I thought maybe there were three of them. I wished I'd gotten a better look.

When I went to turn on the lights, my foot hit the ruined basketball. They knew where Durm lived. So, was it really a suicide gesture or did they hurt him earlier? And why did they come back? Did they think maybe he had something that would identify them? It took me half an hour or so to look through Durmie's place. Worn-out skin magazines were scattered on the floor of his closet along with a smelly towel and another pair of ragged tennies. The hangers were empty and the closet shelf held a partially eaten block of government cheese and a jar of generic peanut butter with the lid off.

A half-empty can of SpaghettiOs on his hot plate had mold in it. Beside it, on top of his dresser, there was a chipped plastic radio with the cord hanging down the side, the plug missing. Probably found it on the street.

I didn't want to look through the drawers but I did, thinking I might find something the punks didn't get to when I interrupted them. Nope. Some clean underwear, candy wrappers, small shiny pieces of broken junk, and several old Ace bandages. Dirty clothes were all over the floor, with the biggest pile humped at the foot of his bed. His sheets were filthy and reeked of sweat and god knows what else.

At the head of his bed, near his pillow that was matted with hair and specks of brownish something-or-other—maybe ooze from scalp sores—stood a night table with a single book. A Bible. Interesting, because I was pretty certain that Durm was illiterate. Maybe it came with the room. I picked it up, curious if it was his, and saw a card stuck about a hundred pages in, like a bookmark. I opened the Bible to that page. No notes or underlining. The card was a wrinkled discount deal from Pizza Heaven, but on the back was a scrawled number—3-6J129. The three might have meant it was a Billings-area license plate. I thought it might match the yellow Chev.

Leaving, when I started down the stairs, I realized my back was sore from hitting the wall. No big deal. I had a day to rest before practice Monday. On the floor below, the Toll Road was standing in the hall again.

"You know those guys?" I asked him as I pushed by.

"What guys?" he said, not looking up. He was smoothing the paper on a cigarette like maybe he had just packed it with something besides tobacco.

Saturday night at the Coulter. No wonder Durmie spent most of his time at the Center.

"DURMOND WILLIAMS. Right in the middle of it," Childress said, underlining something in her small notepad.

"Yeah. He was already in the hospital by then and they were searching his room."

"Why?"

"I'm guessing they thought Durm had something concrete on them. A picture or a packet. Something that linked them with drugs or other crap. And they were right but they didn't find it, I did. I gave the card with the license number to Mom and she was supposed to give it to a c— a policeman."

"So you fought with those guys that night, and this was before they hit a triple with your skull?" Kosich said.

"Yeah. It wasn't much of a fight."

He didn't ask and I didn't volunteer information about having been knocked on my butt and kicked.

"You feel like getting us some sandwiches and a soda or two?" Childress asked.

Kosich nodded and stood.

"How about we have a little food and you tell us the rest of the story how it happened. Chronologically, and we hold the rest of our questions till the end?"

I bit my lip. It was not a story I wanted to tell, but it wasn't a story I wanted rotting inside me either. "I think I could do that," I said.

Childress flicked off the recorder.

13

STALE WHITE BREAD, mystery meat, way too sweet can of iced tea, bag of pretzels. Lunch was so bad I would have preferred a peanut butter sandwich from Durmie's pantry.

Childress was looking at Kosich like she would never again trust him with a food decision.

Kosich was mining his pretzel bag for crumbs.

"Okay," I said, "I don't know what all you know."

Childress leaned over and switched the recorder on. "Everything we said before still applies," she said, watching me to see I understood.

I met her look.

She waited.

"Yes, I understand," I said aloud.

"So, go ahead," she said. "As you please. We'll ask if we can't track it."

Kosich wadded the bag up, pitched it on the table beside the notebooks.

I closed my eyes, took a breath, decided where to start.

"So the new kid, Two Bull, was running and winning every meet. Every meet. And somebody was after him. Seriously. And the hate stuff was being investigated. FBI even, I think. I'm not sure. But the stuff just kept happening."

"This was the locker and the porch thing, the accelerant fire with the animal? And what else? The mess with the running shoes and the feces?" Childress asked, again rifling her notepad for details.

Running shoes? Feces?

AT SCHOOL the halls had been buzzing about Donna's porch fire. Everybody figured it was aimed at Two Bull. Nobody had any guess, any idea who did it. At cross, Coach came and stood in the middle of the locker room. Everybody shut up. Snowfall silent. He looked at each of us in turn. I thought I could see his pulse beat in his forehead and I had a quick picture of him exploding. He never did speak. Turned, walked into his office, and closed the door. Didn't slam it like I expected. That day, I don't think any of us said anything to Danny. His expression didn't invite comment and all of us were uneasy.

The next morning, Friday, at five a.m., the team met in the school parking area and got on the bus for Kalispell four hundred miles away, our longest road trip. Danny usually sat alone behind the coaches in the front of the short bus the school used for the smaller teams: cross, tennis, golf, and so on. I got on right after he did and sat down next to him. He shot me a look, clearly surprised.

I usually sat in the far back with Crane and Sparks and Shugaart, but last night I'd decided to approach Two Bull. Make contact. He was hard to get to know—closed-off, stoic. I could never really tell what he was thinking. He almost always looked a little bit angry, even when he won, but maybe that's just the way kids from his culture carried themselves among strangers. Anyway, I was uncomfortable sitting by him, uncomfortable knowing I was going to talk, intimidated I guess.

He kept his face toward the window, and shortly after the bus rolled out of the parking lot Danny and I went to sleep. Woke up for team lunch of spaghetti and meatballs at a dumpy restaurant just off the freeway in Deer Lodge. After lunch I again sat beside him, and before he could doze, I asked him where he had been in school before. How many students? Any other good athletes? Did his parents ever get to see him run? He gave two- or three-word answers until I asked the parent question and he didn't say anything to that.

I turned a little more in his direction. "I guess I'm pretty bad at making conversation," I said, "but I admire the way you run and the way you carry yourself and I hate the stupid stuff that's been happening." He kept looking out the window but I thought he was listening.

"You might have reason to think that a lot of the kids don't like you because you're the new guy and you're Indian, but it's not true. Either one person or a real small group of morons is behind this shit. The rest of us are embarrassed and, uh . . ." I really didn't know what else to say. "We like you," I finished, and regretted how lame it sounded.

He stayed turned to the window but he spoke. "You think I need you to like me?" he asked. "You think that's why I came to Billings?"

I had the sense to keep my mouth shut.

After what felt like a minute, he turned toward me. "I don't care if people like me."

He looked like he meant it but I didn't know whether I believed it.

"I want to see how good I can run. I want people to know that a goddamned Indian can run them into the ground."

I could feel the heat off his body. I glanced past him out the bus window where barbed fences bordered the highway, where prairie rolled in gray waves toward the mountains.

"And go to college," he said. "I'm going to college. They said nobody'd have me."

"Who said?" I asked, wondering if he meant bigots or school counselors or maybe his parents.

"Well, I'm going," he said. "Bank on it."

We were looking at each other. I think my face was as expressionless as his.

"My girlfriend and I broke up because of a lie I got her to tell," I said. "I couldn't be any bigger asshole." *What am I doing?* "Right now, I guess I wanted you to know that you're not the only one who might feel that the world is pretty sick and stupid."

His eyes blazed. "Sonofabitch!" he exploded. "Now you're gonna tell me your troub—" He shut himself off mid-word, as if a valve had been closed and the steam could no longer get out the pipe. He turned to look out his window again.

I backed off, literally scooted my butt a little closer to the aisle. "Hey, I'm sorry. That's not what I . . . I know you don't want to be friends . . . don't need that, or anything. I guess . . ." I took a breath. "I think I just wanted you to know—" *Well, crap, what did I want him to know?* "That some of us can imagine what it's like to be hazed or bullied and we hate it when it happens to anybody. Particularly to somebody we respect."

I knew it was past time to shut up. I needed to put room between us, but I didn't want to change seats and make it seem like we'd had an argument and that I was leaving in a sulk.

I looked away, out the windows on the other side of the bus. Gray and brown foothills in front of dark ridges. We were past the Tobacco Roots and north of the Sapphires. I liked the different names: the Crazy Woman Mountains, the Big Belts, the Bitterroots. The town we were going to, Kalispell, would be just east of the Salish Range.

"Hey," he said.

I turned back straight ahead, listening but not looking at him.

"I got a hair trigger," he said. "Last night pissed me off."

Out of the corner of my eye it looked like he was facing forward now, too. Like we were watching a movie or a game. We still didn't look at each other.

He leaned to his right and propped his head against the window and went back to sleep.

• • •

KALISPELL IS A TOWN of around twenty thousand in a high desert bowl north of Flathead Lake, not too far from Glacier Park. That day you could see snow covering the surrounding peaks. The temperature was somewhere around fifty but we knew it would get colder near dark, before we finished running.

The Flathead Indian reservation was located on the southwest part of the huge lake and there were lots of Indian service organizations in the nearby area. Coach turned around in his seat and asked Danny if he knew anybody from Kalispell. Danny said no. "Good," Coach said, "then you won't feel bad when you beat them," and turned back around.

Danny did. Ran like a madman. First by at least fifty yards. Me, taking running more seriously, I still had a lot to learn. Since I knew it was going to get colder as we ran, I took a very long warm-up jog. A little too long, a little too fast. Toward the end of the race I didn't have the legs to keep up with Sparks, Shugaart, or even their stubby co-captain. Seventh. But getting there. By the time I'm eighty I'll wow them at the nursing home.

"SO WAS DANNY TWO BULL mad enough to shoot somebody?"

"I don't know. I don't think so. He didn't do it. I told you, I saw what happened."

"We'll get to that," Childress said, crumpling her sandwich wrapper and stuffing it in her soda cup.

"Bet they'll like the sound of that on playback," Kosich said.

Playback. The D.A.

14

I'M HAVING TROUBLE making this fit," Childress said. "Two Bull comes to Billings to run against stronger competition. Hate crimes go against him. Same time, somebody's selling a lot of drugs to street people, more than usual. Did you see a connection?"

"Not at the time," I said. "Not at all. Danny, Raelene, Durmie, none of it made any sense to me."

"Durm . . . Williams sees things around town that lead him to believe the twins are behind the sales. Why does he care?"

"His friends. At the Center," I said. "Some of them are coming unglued doing cheap meth on top of their psych meds. The yellow car, probably selling right there on the corner of State, fifty feet from the ball courts."

"Why doesn't Williams tell the police? Get it stopped?"

"Durmie doesn't rat."

"Okay, so hate crimes and drugs, when did you find out what all was happening at the Rays' house?"

"I didn't see the whole connection till the very end. But I learned more about Raelene and Homer the next time I went out to their place."

"At night."

I nodded.

"Unannounced."

I nodded.

"When?"

"I'm not sure. The week after Kalispell. Somewhere in there."

Kosich had a lined yellow tablet in front of him. I had no idea where he got it. He took a pen out of his pocket and looked at me.

"I couldn't let it alone," I said. "I'd heard my mom talk about this sort of situation. She always said if a person knew some kind of abuse was going on, that somebody was being hurt, the person had a moral obligation to stop it and she as a social worker had a legal obligation to report it. So I felt like I had to find out what was really happening."

I HAD MADE AN EXCUSE to Mom about going to Wib's house for some homework assignments and drove out to Dell about eight-thirty that night. After dark, but I didn't think they'd be in bed yet. Like before, once I started down the far side of the hill there were no dogs barking. The more I thought about it, the stranger that seemed. Near the gully the carrion smell remained but not nearly so strong as the last time. Maybe coyotes had eaten most of it, but this time I needed to check it out. I left the tire tracks and followed a deer trail down a gouge in the ridge as the drainage deepened. The stink got worse and then I was on them. The missing pets. Long dead, piled together, decomposing. I couldn't tell anymore what each had been. My eyes were stinging and I gagged, but I kept looking. Wib's dog could be in there. I pivoted away before I heaved and hiked back to the ruts.

Why hadn't I tipped to this the first time? My mind had been on Raelene. Is there any way this could be legitimate? The burial pit for the dog pound? I was pretty sure they cremated their dead. No. This was so sick I couldn't find words for it. Like some of the war photographs I'd seen and wished I hadn't. I needed to know what else was going on in this asylum. I snuck the rest of the way to the house.

At the porch, I again saw the clothes hanging beside the door and the underthings resting on shoes beneath. I decided to look through the big window on the downhill side, thinking the surroundings would be darker, shaded by a couple of scraggy evergreens. Their indoor lights were on, they wouldn't be able to spot me.

The half-moon I'd seen rising after cross practice was now dulled by a thick layer of stratus. That was in my favor. Problem was my height. I wasn't quite tall enough to see inside over the windowsill. By a run-down shed near the car I found a weathered barrel I could lift and carried it close to the window, setting it at a slight angle where I could see into the main part of the room.

Standing on top of the barrel wasn't going to be as easy as

I had first imagined. It felt tippy. I pushed down on it and twisted it around in the dirt to make it more stable and made a mental note to scuff the round marks I was making before I carried it back to the shed so they wouldn't know it had been set up close to the house. I got on and stood. Better, but still a little teetery. I held my arms out for balance, gradually raised my eyes, and looked through the window.

I could hear a speech, probably coming from a TV that was glowing off to the left but out of my field of vision. I could see most of a square living room with an oval braided rug. In the middle of the rug, facing toward the glow, a sixty- or seventy-year-old man sat stiffly in a straight-backed wooden chair. He looked like a Civil War officer who was one step away from his deathbed. His face was sharpened in a grimace of concentration and his skin looked bleached. He was very thin, wasting away, as if a disease had hold of him. His oily gray hair hung past his shoulders and a surprisingly long brown beard covered most of his face and all of his neck down to the middle of his chest. He wore a long-sleeved khaki shirt and his bony wrists stuck out the cuffs and rested on his knees. Similar khaki pants looked almost like a uniform, and his leather boots came over his calves.

Past him to the right I could see a guy about my age sitting on a three-legged stool facing the far corner of the room like a kid being punished in kindergarten. There was a standing lamp near him and he was reading a math textbook that looked familiar. Homework. He had on cheap cloth slippers. I could see pimples on his back and his butt. The far wall was partly obscured by a ratty sofa and some bookcases, and the back of the room was split by a lit doorway. While I was studying it—the kitchen, I thought—Raelene walked by the open door carrying a tray and a dish towel and disappeared right to left. Nothing on.

LATER I GUESSED maybe an owl sailed by me right then, or maybe the wood in the barrel shifted, but whatever the cause, I lost my balance and fell. I don't know if I cried out, but my tumble and the old staves breaking made noise. I lit out running for the hill and in three or four seconds I heard someone yelling from the porch. I sprinted, wondering if they could see well enough to shoot me. What would they do? The kid would have to get dressed before he could chase me. The older guy looked too feeble to run. I didn't think they'd call the cops out to their scene, whatever it was, so they would probably come after me in the car. I should have thought of that.

Okay, the gully or the road. If I did the gully, they'd find my beat-up Land Cruiser and figure out who'd been spying. I could reach my car in about a minute, probably have enough time to start it and get moving. I tore over the crest and down the hill as fast as I could without falling. I got my car started first try and looked to the hill for headlights. None yet. They'd expect me to head for town. I put it in reverse and backed as fast as I could toward Dell and the derelict gas station. Kept my lights off and my foot off the brakes. It was probably a good idea, but in my hurry I lost control, shot off the pavement, and slid down into the weedy furrow on my side of the road. I wound up stopped in tall grass next to a fence. In that last moment I had seen the Taurus leap the crest of the hill, rocket down the ruts to the blacktop, and make a fishtailing left turn toward town. As far as I knew, whoever was in the Ford didn't even look in my direction. My car had stalled and I could hear how hard I was breathing.

I knew I was pretty desperate because my first thought was to bury the car so they couldn't find it. Even *I* realized that wasn't exactly brilliant. I got out to see how bad I was stuck. I had plowed a bunch of soft dirt and tall grass behind my back wheels and that's what had stopped me. The front was pretty clear. I didn't think I could get the traction to climb back to the road the way I'd slid off, but if the car would move forward, I was sure I could get up enough steam to climb the bank down a ways where the grade wasn't so steep. I put it in four-wheel-drive. It worked.

Back on the two-lane, I took it out of 4WD, pulled on the emergency brake, and got out to see if I could cover the damage so tomorrow they wouldn't see where I'd hidden. Nope. My skid had torn the grass and weeds beyond repair. So now what? If I drove to town, I ran the risk of meeting them on the road. Where did this Dell road go? Did it connect to anywhere?

I made a U-turn and headed farther west around the big looping curve past the ghost town. There was a long straightaway ahead. I kept my lights off. At the beginning of the next curve I stopped where I could see if any cars were coming behind me and found my flashlight in the door pocket. I carried maps in my glove compartment, and the Yellowstone County one showed the road I was on went northwest toward Rapelje for several miles and then crossed another one that went northeast toward Acton and Highway 3 south to home. It might take an hour or so but it was safe. I gunned it and decided to keep my headlights off unless I saw an oncoming car.

Down the road I found myself hyperventilating. Had I ever been so scared? I had thought if they caught me, they would shoot me. Probably. Anybody might kill to preserve a secret like that. The dead pets. And the home: clothes on the porch, the kids naked inside the house. I knew the pet killing was against the law, and the pervert thing? That had to be, too. It ought to be. It better be. Raelene and her brother trapped in a home with that sicko. How crazy was he? What did he force them to do? I had to report this as soon as I got home. The pet grave. They'd put him in jail for that. In prison. For years. But even as I thought it, I knew I couldn't do it. The sheriff's department or the highway patrol would flood in and catch him. And see Raelene and her brother naked. They'd throw away the key on that weirdo but everyone would know. You can't hide a secret like that. Everybody would find out Raelene had been kept naked. It would ruin her. I didn't think she could take it. I wasn't sure what she would do. Maybe—

I heard my tires screeching and stepped on the brakes. I'd been going way too fast on a sharp bend. I took a deep breath, put my lights on, and made myself slow down. That's what I needed to do: slow down. Think up a better plan.

In a few minutes I saw the sign marking my turnoff.

15

THE WEIRDO, the ex-guru, was Raelene and Homer's real father, right? They weren't just some kids he took in?" Childress asked, looking at Kosich for confirmation. "The girl's halfway normal, the brother's a year younger, on his way to be Hannibal Lecter, right?"

Kosich was nodding. "Yeah, the old man's their dad. And the brother's a sicko. Acorn and oak."

"I wonder if the old man's crazy," Childress said. "Maybe drug-damaged. LSD. We'll find out."

Kosich had stopped writing. He'd already finished at least a couple of pages of notes, and I could see he'd made a sketch of a room. The Guru's house? Why? What was he thinking? Was this going to be used against me?

"Bought that place, Dell, back in the early eighties," Kosich said. "Incredible. The commune and the symposiums. Brought people from all over Montana, some from Idaho, some all the way from California."

"Nowadays the Feds would raid it. Bust the cult," Childress said.

"Even though they were doing some good things?" I said.

"Probably," Childress said. "Let's keep going."

"Your mom's Maya James? Social Worker at Buchanan Center?" Kosich said.

It really wasn't a question.

"What was she doing during your shenanigans?" he asked.

"Well, she blew up a couple of days after that second Ray house visit, when I had to tell her about the Anita thing."

DUSK HAD TURNED OUR WHITE HOUSE GRAY and the green shutters black when I pulled up the short hill into our carport. I had expected Mom to have dinner waiting. I was surprised to see her sitting in the living room when I opened the front door.

"Pee if you need to and wash your hands," she said, looking up from the book she was reading. "We're going to eat at Smokey's."

Barbecue sounded good. And Mom probably wanted to talk. When we ate at home, we usually shoveled it in, washed the dishes, and headed to our own business. When we ate out, we usually paid more attention to each other. That and driving on a long trip were our traditional times to give a personal report. Drying my hands, I looked in the mirror and didn't like what I saw. I remembered I still hadn't really talked to Mom about the breakup with Anita. I didn't want to. And I sure didn't want to talk about Raelene.

I couldn't think of an excuse to get out of going, so I joined her in the living room. "My car or yours?" I asked.

She put the book down on the marble-topped end table. "Mine. My invitation, my treat."

Right.

Once she backed out the driveway, she began. "Gabriel, I feel just a little bit like I've been running a bed-and-breakfast for you lately. I feed you, do your laundry, go to your cross-country meets, and stand by while you tell me hello and good-bye. You really haven't said boo for weeks since the night that Chavez girl called, and I want to hear what's been going on with you, what's been going on at school, and whatever you know about the Center. You think about it while I'm driving, and once we get there and order, I expect you to fill me in. Clear?"

"Clear," I said, and wondered whether or not I would tell her the truth.

SMOKEY'S WAS A CINDER-BLOCK RECTANGLE painted brick red, serving the only decent Kansas City–style barbecue in our county. The tables were surfaced with that hard gray stuff, Formica, and the seats were chrome with padding for the butt and back. A no-frills kind of place. We each ordered a half-rack with beans and slaw, one hot link to share. When the waitress left, Mom folded her hands in front of her on the table.

I waited until after the waitress returned with our napkins and silverware and set our tall Dr Peppers beside our plates.

"Um . . ." I couldn't decide where to start. I looked at

Mom. She had that I-can-wait-patiently-until-the-next-ice-age expression.

"Uh, before school started . . ."

She didn't interrupt.

"I didn't go visit another guitar player in Butte like I told you." I had been looking at my soda but I glanced up to see how she was taking that news. No change. Waiting, listening.

"I . . . instead I went on a little road trip, fishing and stuff with Anita out around Red Lodge." Glanced again. Maybe her eyes were a little narrower. "And her folks, uh, her dad actually, found out about it and forbid her to see me anymore."

Man, I really wanted to be done with this. I willed for the food to arrive, or old friends to walk in, or the fire alarm to go off.

"And," my mom said. She still hadn't changed position.

"And, uh, and I'm sorry I lied to you but . . . but I didn't think you'd let me go if I told you the truth, or I thought you might call her folks, or something that would mess it up, and I really wanted to do it, so, I lied." That felt awful to say. The words coiled on the table between us like a snake.

Neither of us moved. I could hear blurred conversation at other tables and plates clanking in the kitchen. "And so I, um, I couldn't tell you, right? Because you would be ashamed of me and I'm all you have after Dad and, and I couldn't do that to you."

Mom's hand hit the table with a *crack* that startled everyone in the restaurant. She leaned over and hissed at me so nobody else could catch what she was saying.

"That is the most cowardly crap I've ever heard leave your mouth, Gabriel James! You want to try that again?"

Whoa! I don't know if I had ever seen Mom so mad. At least, not at me. I may have been stammering but I don't think anything like a word came out.

She leaned across the table even closer. If there had been a snake there before, she would have scared it into oblivion. She whispered slowly and distinctly.

"You didn't tell me because it would expose your lie and you were ashamed of yourself. I understand that, but it was gutless. You think us human beings don't sometimes make big mistakes?"

She kept leaning and maybe I had backed up an inch or two.

"And, Gabriel, you are the most important person in my life. Always will be. But—you—are—not—my—life." Every word punctuated with a gesture, hammering the point. "I have a life. With people that love me. And I have work that I believe in. I respect myself and I choose what I do. Do—you—understand?"

I think I was nodding yes.

"Good," she said, leaning back. "No one is *all I have.* Got it?"

I said yes.

"Good." She put her hands back out on the table in front of her. "Now," she said, "what else?"

I had to start breathing again. When I had sucked in a couple of lungfuls, I went on.

"Well, I've been pretty sad and lonesome without her, Anita . . . I really liked her. Not just physically I mean." I could feel that snake on the table again, but I kept going. "So, it's not like I'm looking for a girlfriend now, but, but I wouldn't mind one, I guess. And, uh, and at school, after the fire on the Plenty Waters' porch . . . you knew about that, right? . . . somebody put a dead dog in Danny's team locker at school . . . not just dead, uh, gross, reeking. And it was gone when the police came to get it from the Dumpster? Did I tell you about that? But nothing has happened to Danny since then, that I know of, and Wibby told me that a girl in my class liked me and I followed her home and she left all her clothes on a hook outside her front door, bra and everything, and so did her brother . . ." I was getting a message from my brain. *Time to shut up now!*

I stopped and looked up at her.

She had moved back from the table. Her mouth was open a little and her face was redder. She looked like she was going to say something any minute, but she didn't. Seemed like the snake had slithered off and a spaceship had landed in its place.

The waitress came and put a platter of ribs right on top of it and the spell was broken. We just ate for a while. Mom kept looking like she was going to say something, but each time I guess she decided against it. Me, I'd said more than enough. I kept my mouth full of food.

On the ride home, she asked questions and I answered them. When she turned the engine off in our carport, neither of us got out. The questions continued. I told her what Durmie had said about the Center, the possibility that outsiders, the blond guys, yellow Chevy, were selling street drugs to the mentally ill. I had told her about following the girl and I asked her if she had ever heard of such a thing, naked at home.

She asked if I was certain they were nude inside the house, just the kids, not the adults, too, because if they were, she would probably need to file a report. She said perhaps they were some kind of religious sect or some kind of naturist group and didn't feel clothes were necessary inside, said that keeping the body covered at all times hadn't always been as important as it seemed nowadays. But making teenagers go naked while clothed adults were present needed investigation. Sounded like child abuse.

I lied again. Told her I wasn't really sure. Told her I'd find out right away.

"DID SHE KNOW you were going back out there?" Childress asked.

"No. I never told her. I didn't tell anybody."

"Why didn't you come to us about the pet grave?" Childress was tapping her pen on the table, forehead creased. She thought I was hiding something. Was she reacting to what I'd just said, or the way I'd said it?

"I . . . It didn't seem like the right thing. I, uh, even if I did think of it, it wouldn't work. Like I said, the naked thing would come out. That's why I couldn't tell Mom. She'd go right to you. I thought about telling Crane, but I hadn't been so close to him lately and maybe he'd tell Genelle and then it would be all over school. Wib . . . he's a good guy, but I couldn't see how he could help. Who was I supposed to go to? What was I supposed to do?"

16

WHAT HAVE WE MISSED SO FAR?" Childress asked.

"I got to stretch," Kosich said, standing.

"Need to leave? Take a break?"

"Not yet. Close. Fifteen minutes."

"You?" Childress looked at me.

I needed to pee but I didn't say so. Anything to get this over and be done.

"Okay, we got guys selling drugs to street people, we got an Indian kid with a target on his back, we got a zoo out at Dell. What's the thread that holds it all together?"

"Nobody saw it," I said. "But I'm pretty sure it was Homer. He ran the twins."

"Hold a minute while I check something," Childress said, reaching for the stack of notebooks. "Won't take long. Nobody found any more of Homer's writings, did they? The car? The shed? Just these four journals?" she asked Kosich.

He shrugged.

She made a quick search of the third notebook in the stack. "When did you know that Homer also called himself Doctor Death, MDD?" Childress asked, setting that journal in front of her and picking up the bottom one.

"Not until later," I said. "Why MDD?"

"MD, doctor, D, death," Childress said, thumbing pages, stopping to look more closely at the ones with folded corners.

"Yeah, right, the Manifesto. I told you that Emily said he called himself something strange. I didn't know him. Never heard Homer speak that I can remember until that last night."

"Was it Hornet?" Childress asked me.

"The name? No. I never heard that one." I shook my head. "Emily never remembered. She pretty much thought all their names were odd."

"That was another one of the boy's secrets. I don't think . . . he didn't let anybody know he had other identities, personalities," Childress said, raised her eyebrows at Kosich.

Kosich yawned.

"Listen to this." Childress referred to her own small notepad: "Homer says he doesn't know where Hornet comes from. Says he, Homer, can call him out, ask for him, but he doesn't have to come. Hornet's on his own. He's real. Not like Hawk. Not like MDD the revenger. Says Hornet rules. Hornet can keep stinging, and stinging, and stinging. He doesn't have to stop."

"All this third-person stuff, and then sometimes he jumps to the next level, actually becomes another person," Kosich said. "So the kid was getting more split apart. Hawk and MDD were like, what do you call it?"

"An alias?" Childress supplied.

"I don't think so. Not something to avoid prosecution. More like stage names. Characters he invented to seem stronger or more mysterious. But Hornet? Very serious. The kid didn't have control over that one. Or not conscious control. From what he says, Hornet would . . . take the kid over? Multiple-identity kind of thing."

"Multiple?" I asked.

"Multiple personality," Childress said. "May be a response to repeated abuse. Post-traumatic stress thing. Very controversial. Is it a real alternate identity or is it a manipulation . . ."

"You remember the Shay bust? Were you working here then?" Kosich asked.

"Shay?"

"Phillip Shay? Pedophile? Kept that boy in a . . . Anyway, kidnapped a kid, held him for almost a year until the kid escaped."

"I think his trial was going on when I started," Childress said.

"So you know who Shay was?"

"Slime."

"Yeah. And Vernon Ray's accountant."

Childress gave him her full attention.

"Shay was the last to leave the compound. Stayed on till the end and, after Ray's second wife left him, lived with Ray and the kids for three or four years when they were pretty young. Had a thing for boys but was real slick, real cagey. Possible he got to Homer without Sun Ray knowing. Tell-and-I'll-hurt-your-sister kind of thing."

Childress was rigid. I could see the muscles tightening in her jaw. Kosich had stopped talking and had gone still. I could hear us breathe.

"Multiple personality," Childress said, breaking the silence. "That might explain it." She flipped the recorder off and left the room.

"Guess it's time for that break," Kosich said. He stood, wiped at his nose. "Maybe I'll hit the can," he said. "You?"

"Yeah," I said. "I could do that."

Walking down the hall behind Kosich, I kept wondering if this was another tactic on their part. Decided I wouldn't say anything in the bathroom.

"DID ANYBODY EVER CHECK to see if Homer was the given name on the birth certificate?" Kosich asked, writing again when we were back at the table.

"I didn't hear if they did," Childress answered. She'd come back all business. Turned on the recorder and pushed the notebook in front of her over to the main stack. "Anybody call Danny Two Bull a rat?"

I looked at her. Realized the question was directed to me. Seemed like ten minutes ago the two of them were practically ignoring me. Was *that* more maneuvering on their part? I couldn't decide if or how they were playing me. "No," I said. "I never heard that."

"What did Homer call Two Bull?"

"I don't know."

"Did you hear the kid call the twins his rats . . . good rats? My rats?"

I shook my head. I didn't like hearing this stuff. Made my skin crawl.

"Did you know Homer and the twins were partners?" Childress asked.

"The Trinity," Kosich said.

I couldn't tell if that was supposed to be funny.

"Not till the last night," I said. That reminded me of the knot on my head. I made myself not touch it, not draw their attention to it. Didn't want them to see me as a loser.

"In here somewhere he talks about the twins' father hitting them with their own bats. Little League." Childress gestured toward the notebooks.

"The junkyard owner? Had practically a pharmacy on his property?" Kosich reached toward the stack of notebooks.

"It's not in there," Childress said. Found what she wanted in her own notes. "The twins' dad? A lab? Yeah. Arrested the morning after. Production/distribution of meth, possession and sales of controlled substances, painkillers, benzos, you name it. Jurgen Dersch. Five priors plus a laundry list of parole violations. Divorced. So it was Jurgen, Jules, and Judd out at the junkyard. J-birds. Must have been a cozy nest."

"Didn't the twins get their product from him?" Kosich asked.

"At first. The speed and some sleepers anyway, until they branched out," Childress said.

"Family values," Kosich said, moving his tongue around his teeth like he could use a toothpick.

Kosich was really starting to aggravate me. Sarcastic, detached, cynical, most of the time he couldn't give a damn, then he's writing a book. What's the deal?

"And this," Childress returned to her notes. "You know how they got the pets?"

I said no.

"Know anything about the tranqs, the crossbow? The so-called people? Ever hear someone call the hate crimes 'stinging'?"

"Don't keep going over that stuff," Kosich said. "Make you move to Antarctica."

"All the pet killing's outlined except the names and addresses," Childress said, picking up an earlier notebook.

"The twins go to your school?" she asked.

"No."

"According to this, the twins turned MDD on to the Indian," she said to no one in particular. "Are the twins or Jurgen linked with an Aryan bunch?" Childress asked Kosich.

"Bet the dad is," Kosich said. "Jurgen. Bet the kids got it from him. The Brotherhood here spews the same shit as the Klan down south. Just change the race."

"These don't say anything about white supremacy," Childress said.

"I don't think the Ray kid would join any group. He's a king with a kingdom of two, like his dad turned out," Kosich said.

I was trying to follow this. The Guru's kingdom had whittled down to his two kids and with Homer it was sort of the same thing with the twins?

"Sounds right," Childress said, looking away toward the corner of the room like she was putting things together.

Kosich continued. "Homer comes across hating anyone who was different like he was but who was actually successful. Two Bull's instant fame as a runner must have really fried him. Outsider makes good. Just like Homer, naked boy, would never be able to do."

Again he was talking to Childress and seemed to be thinking aloud at the same time. Had he forgotten I was in the room?

Childress coughed and he came out of it. Grimaced when he saw me looking at him.

"Guess we'll never know," Childress said, seeming to close the topic. "So." She thumbed through her notes again. "Wait a minute. There's this about Two Bull. 'Red Dog thinks he's too cool but he's not even real. He is the old form but not emitting' . . . What's he talking about? Form? Emitting? What does he mean?"

Now I was really confused. Earlier she had practically shushed Kosich when he picked up the journals and now she's reading some quote from her notes? What happened? Did she have a quick meeting with him while I'd been back in here alone for a couple of minutes after the bathroom? I couldn't sense what was going on. Was she acting this way to make it seem like we were all figuring this out together and then trap me? Was that too paranoid? And what about the mirror . . . was she actually trying to shield him from saying something that would get him in trouble?

Kosich was shaking his head. "Form, emitting . . . Sun Ray gave all those speeches about Forms and the Ideal. Put all this Plato stuff in a current package. That's what's on those videos that he kept listening to. His Saturday Night Talks. How we had to shake off the Culture of Self and get back to the Ideal. The kid latched on to some of the gobbledygook. Ray used to say something . . . 'we need to emit love like the sun.'"

"How do you know all this stuff?" I asked him. I was starting to have a theory that went like this: He was there for some of the commune thing. Actually involved. He didn't necessarily want to say so directly because of the recorder. Maybe his superiors didn't know that about him. Maybe it was none of their business now, so many years later. But he wanted to fill Childress in, and at some point she got what was happening and . . . and what? Maybe that didn't make any sense.

He snorted, dismissed my question. Countered with one of his own. "You said one of Homer's jobs was to drive her, Raelene, back and forth to school?"

"I don't know if I said it. I saw it, remember, when I fol—" I cut myself off. Didn't want to get back to the stalking conversation.

"Probably how he got access for some of the vandalism like the trophy case and Two Bull's locker. Him or Crane," Kosich said, continuing to fit the pieces.

I winced. I didn't want to picture Crane doing things like that.

Childress was tapping the top notebook with her pen. "He says how this home no-clothes thing began to drive him crazy after his sister started filling out a little."

"He was already crazy," Kosich said.

"He talks about how at least his dad kept them, cared for them, after the different women moved out. About how his dad was always trying to teach them things, pass on his philosophy. Sun Ray, what was his real name?" Childress asked.

"Vernon. I told you. Vernon Ray. He changed it to Sun years ago." Kosich sounded irritated that Childress couldn't keep these details straight.

"Somehow this Platonic philosophy gets bent into shaming, humiliating, old-fashioned sit-in-a-corner discipline," she said, rolling her eyes.

"I saw that," I said. "Homer in the corner naked."

"So as the Guru deteriorates, he gets more into control, Homer gets more desperate," Childress said, standing and pacing between the table and the door. "The kid starts talking about how much he loves his sister, wants to protect her. Says he's stopped planning to kill his dad because his dad would be dead soon enough. But he's wondering if Hornet will come to stay full-time, talking about shooting, burning, bringing everything down." She stopped pacing to look at Kosich. "Did you read his dream?"

Kosich made no response.

"Same one, over and over again." Childress came back to the table, found another marked page, and handed it to Kosich. "Flying car . . . ejecting Dad like a bomb . . . mushroom clouds . . . drowning in jellyfish," she prompted.

Kosich located it with his finger.

Childress nodded. Kosich shook his head.

"I feel bad for this kid, for what he had to endure," Childress went on. "Seriously. But no matter how you slice it, he was lethal. Doctor Death. And he was getting worse. Hornet's 'ascending the throne.' Now that's—"

But Kosich interrupted. "That's enough," he said, and silence washed in as the three of us listened while the sound of the old-fashioned wall clock grew louder, the seconds ticking by like the hammering of a gavel.

17

OKAY, WHERE WERE WE?" Childress had dealt with the lunch trash, tidied the table, squared the stack of notebooks.

Kosich was seated at the end, perpendicular to her.

During the lull I had been walking around the room, looking at myself briefly in the two-way mirror. I wanted to ask if there was anybody behind there but I didn't want to seem nervous or paranoid.

I sat once again, across from them. "Is my mom back there?" It was out before I even knew I'd been thinking it.

Kosich answered. "No."

"So you were going to tell us step by step but we keep getting sidetracked," Childress said, shepherding.

More than sidetracked, I was lost. Much the same way I had been as this thing ran its course. "Um, I told you the naked stuff, Two Bull winning despite the attacks, me wanting to help Raelene and getting interested in Emily, and uh, the running, taking it seriously."

"I used to run," Childress said. "Four-forty in high school, eight hundred for a while in college."

I didn't know what to say to that.

"You?" she asked, looking to Kosich.

"Football," Kosich said. "Nose tackle. A grunt. Okay at the time."

If this was supposed to make me feel closer to them, it didn't work. "Did I talk about Crane not running as well as the season went on? He still usually came in second but his times were getting worse. He blamed it on a bruised heel and stopped practicing as hard. It really messed with him that he couldn't beat Two Bull."

"But now we know there was more to it," Childress said. "We'll come back to him. Let's close Emily out."

Kosich shut his eyes, folded his hands in his lap, resting or annoyed again. I couldn't tell.

"Okay," I said, "Emily. I kept trying to get her to step up or at least help me help Raelene. I finally told her there was a reason Raelene didn't want her to visit."

I CAUGHT HER in the hall again before cross practice. "Here's the deal. She and her brother don't wear clothes while they're at home," I said, whispering so others in the hall couldn't hear. "But their dad stays dressed and he looks really goofy, really defective. Raelene and her brother are caught up in something totally twisted."

At first her eyes widened and then they narrowed, angry

again. "You've been spying on her?" she accused. "That's despicable!" She turned to walk again.

"Hold up!" I said, louder than I meant to. "Just a second." I quieted. "I only went out there to get to know her better. I saw her and her brother's clothes, all of them, hanging outside the front door. I ran the first time, but then I went back another time because I thought maybe I'd gotten the wrong idea."

I took half a step closer to her so people walking by couldn't hear. "So her dad sits watching TV but she and her brother weren't wearing anything. The brother was studying naked and she was doing dishes naked. Does that sound right to you? The brother was sitting on a stool in the corner, facing the wall like a first grader. The dad's a sick puppy. Not just mentally. He's rail thin. Whatever's going on, it shouldn't be happening."

Emily's arms were crossed in front of her like they could block this information, her face set in a grimace.

I kept talking. "I don't know who else to tell this to. If I go to an adult they'll report it and then, before long, everybody will know. I don't want that. I know you don't." I stopped and kept my eyes up and let her look at me.

"You're making me sick," she said.

She left me standing there.

"THE BEGINNING OF THE END is when Raelene screamed," I said, fighting my way out of those thoughts.

"Screamed? When?" Childress was surprised.

I even had Kosich's attention.

"*Where* is more important. At school. In English class."

RAELENE WAS CONTINUING to stonewall me. I was being careful, polite. I tried to make like a formal appointment with her when there were breaks between book reports. She wouldn't look at me, wouldn't respond, so I cornered her after class and she lost it. She actually screamed. Loud. And when Mr. Hopgood came over to break us up, I didn't know what to say. She told him that I had been pestering her about a date for weeks and that I wouldn't take no for an answer. Some other kids, rubberneckers, heard her say that. Gabe stalking the shyest girl in school. Gross.

First I was angry. I didn't deserve that. But then I was humiliated. Neither Mr. Hopgood nor anyone else listened when I tried to explain. Trying to help her? Right. Everybody'd probably seen me trying to get her attention lately. I knew her accusation would arc through the school at the speed of light. Mr. Hopgood was shaking his head before I finished my first sentence.

"Don't make excuses, Gabe." Hopgood had stepped between us. "Harassing, menacing a young woman is abuse of power just like racism, and it's utterly and completely unacceptable. Don't ever do it again here at school or anywhere else. I mean it."

He walked Raelene to the door and waited until she was out of sight before motioning for me to leave his classroom.

I decided to give it a couple of days before trying another explanation. Maybe if I wrote it he'd listen.

The scream had already made the news. In the hall, Genelle shot me a look, people I didn't know moved away from me. Lately I'd been asking everybody about Raelene. Clearly interested in her. Now everyone would instantly take her side, thinking I'd gone way too far. Gotten obsessed. *Had I?* Of course they'd want to defend her. I would have, too, if it were someone else doing what people thought I was doing.

I wasn't mad at Raelene. I understood. She was trying to prevent her own humiliation, protect her privacy, and cover up whatever weird crap went on out in Dell. I knew she saw talking to me as a lose-lose situation, and I knew it was even a little worse because at one time she had been attracted to me. But I was frustrated. Major League frustrated.

And I thought about Emily. I wanted to be the one to tell her about this recent mess with Raelene, wanted her to hear my side first. After every class I searched the halls. Was this one of her work-study days? Was she out on a special project? I never found her. And then it was time for cross practice.

AFTER DINNER I helped Mom clean up the dishes. I could have told her about the misunderstanding at school, could have told her more specifics about Raelene and the dad and the brother, but I . . . I what? I guess I thought the information wouldn't do her any particular good. She'd forbid me to do anything else and call the school, or maybe even put the whole story together and call Protective Services. It seemed like that would make everything worse for everybody.

I could get it that sometimes things had to get worse before they got better, like a junkie has to put up with being sick in order to get heroin out of his system, or a beat-on woman has to go through hell to get away from a violent husband. So, my main trouble? I realized I still didn't know *for sure* what was really going on with the Rays. The pets, yeah, but I believed that would only involve the father or the brother. What if the naked thing was totally different than I thought? What if the dad wasn't forcing them? What if I was missing something and there was a real reason for it, like some allergy or a weird health condition? I didn't think so, I didn't, but I wasn't dead certain, and I couldn't stand to detonate that bomb if I wasn't positive. If I ruined Raelene's life by mistake, for basically nothing, how would I live it down? And more selfishly I wondered, who would ever like me again? I'd go back to feeling hollow. Maybe for good.

But I wish I had told Mom. It might have made a difference. Maybe she would have recognized the family, or warned me and maybe I would have listened.

Fat chance.

Instead I gave her the card with the license plate number I'd found in Durmie's room. "Would you give that to one of the policemen that come to the Center? I got it from a friend and I think it's the number of a yellow Chevy that's been selling street drugs to the mentally ill."

"SO YOU KEEP YOUR MOM in the dark about everything you do?" Kosich asked.

Now Kosich is going to show some concern? "No," I said, "but the things I mess up, I try to fix. Are you trying to not understand?"

Kosich looked away, frowning.

"I knew I was right about the missing pets, but the Raelene thing had to be handled really, really carefully. Like I think I told you, I had to be sure. I wanted proof about who did the pet killing and what the no-clothes stuff really was before I told Mom. I didn't know about the racial hatred stuff until the Manifesto appeared. If I told Mom, I knew as soon as I did, Mom would tell you guys, and Raelene's story would explode all over town. Her life would never be the same and I didn't think she could handle it. What if she hurt herself? Telling Mom, telling anybody else was a last resort."

"Why didn't you come to us as soon as you found the pets?" Kosich wouldn't let it go.

"How many times do I have to—?"

"You have to say it till it makes sense!" Kosich said. The room echoed.

"I was alone with this," I said, my own voice rising. "There was no one to tell, nowhere to go with it except Emily, and she—" I could feel water forming in the back of my eyes. No way. I coughed hard so I could wipe my face.

Kosich snorted again and I wanted to slug him. He didn't know me. What's with his attitude? Was there a theory that if you made someone angry enough they'd blurt out information they'd been holding? Or did dealing with criminals for years breed some kind of permanent disdain? He seemed almost bored when we started, then he's a historian, and now he's pissed about something? Was this shape-shifter stuff intentional? Was it supposed to rattle me into making a mistake? Is it possible he messed up this investigation and now he's all over the place trying to cover it up? Is he involved somehow?

I snuck a look at him. He was staring me down. Whatever, I needed to chill before I said something foolish. My plan coming in. Answer the questions, don't add anything, don't drop your guard.

"Sure, I was scared about what was going on. I knew it was serious. Really serious. But I wasn't ready. I didn't want to be the one to expose her. Some people already thought I was stalking her. This would make it even kinkier. *Gabe gets off spying on her naked*." I shuddered and clamped it off. "I just wanted to help."

"I guess I can understand that reasoning," Childress said, "but it was costly. Those two deaths didn't have to happen."

That felt worse than the baseball bat I got to the side of the head.

I slogged on with the telling. "So I was home that night listening to Mom talking about how hard our economy is on the homeless and mentally ill."

SHE'D SAID most don't have any family they can count on and no money at all. Said the fortunate ones get a disability check that covers rent with fifteen or twenty dollars a month left over for food and what have you.

We were interrupted by my cell phone.

Emily.

"I looked all over for you today," I said.

"I owe you some money."

"Five dollars," I said, "but who's counting?"

"That isn't why I called," she said. "I talked to Raelene between classes today. She told me she's going to ask to be homeschooled. She felt it was too hard on her to live in both worlds."

"Did you tell her you knew about the naked thing?"

"No. I couldn't. That would make it even worse. Then she'd be too ashamed to be around me and she wouldn't have anybody she could talk to."

"Yeah, but homeschooled means she'd be in that hellhole all the time. Her brother's homeschooled."

"I guess you can get used to anything," Emily said. "And there's something else."

"What?"

"I can't keep . . . I wish I didn't know all this. I hate carrying secrets, especially this. It's too ugly. Sometimes I wish I'd never . . . I wish you hadn't brought this stuff to me. Everything's so complicated. And you. I don't even know what to do with you."

I didn't know what to say to that. I wondered if my wanting to fix things actually made it worse for everybody. Durmie. Raelene.

"You're like Typhoid Mary," Emily said, apparently thinking along with me. "You get involved in some cause and go to help and everybody near you gets sick with what you carry."

I wanted to hold the phone away from my ear.

"In a way, Raelene wouldn't even be upset if it weren't for you. And I don't think she could take it knowing that you'd seen her that way, and that you were telling other people about her. She'd die of shame. Ick! . . . I can't talk about this anymore."

The silence following her words got louder and louder.

Finally she said, "I have to go," and hung up.

I clicked the phone off and stood in the hall thinking about what she'd said. Was she right? Would everything be better off without me? Why exactly was I trying to help? Did I really care, or did I do it so I could feel good about myself? I had no answer. I didn't understand it. I did it because I had to.

I knew about Typhoid Mary. She was stubborn and not very educated and she couldn't believe that she was contaminating others with an illness she didn't suffer from. She thought the doctors and police were wrong about her and she continued to cook for other families until authorities put her away. People died and more were infected. I was stubborn. But was I a menace?

18

WHEN WAS THIS, this Emily call? Is this the final time you went back to Dell?" Childress asked.

"No, this was Monday a week ago, I guess. Tuesday I was a pariah at school. I wasn't sure how long it would last. Everybody felt sorry for Raelene and avoided me like I was a degenerate, a couldn't-take-'no' stalker. I stayed away from Wib and Crane and Victor so the stink wouldn't rub off on them and I didn't run into Raelene or Emily. Finally, when I asked in the office, Mrs. Spengle was curt. 'I haven't seen either of them' was all she would say, giving me the evil eye."

AT CROSS PRACTICE THAT AFTERNOON, Coach emphasized State was going to be in Butte that coming Saturday. He reminded us we'd made it through the season losing only once over a month ago, on points, to Missoula. I'd placed in three of the last five meets. Coach was telling us that we'd been improving and that we had our chance to win it all.

More than that, I knew they counted every place for the top five team members with the sixth best being a tiebreaker if needed. The better I ran, the better our team score. I could finally contribute something important. If all five of us—Two Bull, Crane, Sparks, Shugaart, and I—placed in the top forty, there was a chance we'd win it.

After cross I'd gone to the hospital. The good news: Durmie was out of the I.C.U. The bad news: he was heavily sedated and the charge nurse said he couldn't have any visitors. I pleaded that I was the one who found him, one of his best friends. She told me he was still threatening suicide and that he couldn't be managed in an acute medical care hospital like this one. She thought when his fever dropped they would transfer him to the state psych hospital right away. She said she knew from past experience that once he started obsessing on suicide, he usually didn't let up until he got admitted to Warm Springs. She was shaking her head.

"I never met anyone else who wanted to be in a mental hospital so badly," she said.

I thought about how Durmie had described Warm Springs. He made it seem like a summer camp with games and activities and partners to fleece. And it would be safe. I knew he was ready for safe.

"Will you be here when they come for him?" I asked her.

"I expect so."

"Before he goes, would you tell him I was here to see him and I can't wait to kick his ass in Around-the-World when he comes back?"

THE INTERROGATION OF GABRIEL JAMES

"I DON'T KNOW IF YOU'LL BELIEVE ME, but that night I was ready to drop the whole thing."

Childress raised her eyebrows again. Kosich took a bigger breath than usual.

"Durmie was going to be okay. I'd inadvertently deflected attention from whatever was happening to Raelene. I was thinking it was time to give everything I had to running for once, and let the other stuff go. Maybe not forget about it, but step away from it. Raelene wanted me to, whether or not that was really in her best interest. Emily had already ducked out. Danny and the police could handle the hate stuff, and I'd mind my own business."

Typhoid Gabriel could go to rehab.

I could have done it, too. I think. Except for the Manifesto.

WEDNESDAY AT LUNCH the students heading off campus found flyers under their windshield wipers. White copy paper with black print.

MANIFESTO

The first truth, the ONLY TRUTH, is that we are all alike. All humans beings are part of the ideal world of forms. Everything is a form. When some people try to be different, they are going against the Universe. They must be brought to line. Here the first people who tried to be different were indians. Look what it got them. Now every indian must be taught that he is the same as all of us. If they try to stand away, they must be relined. And so the others, the socalled African People, the socalled Arabian people, all are the same as us or not at all. People who are alike are perfect as we are. Like people can emit love. We do not need to be worshiped. We do not need animals to worship us. Dogs aren't animals. They have been born to become deciples. That is idolatry and can never be tolerated. We are alike but many of us have been blinded by a stupid upbringing. These blinded must be awake. That is the Doctors job.

See and you will wake. Follow and be rewarded.

Breath in the true light.

Doctor Death. MDD.

It was the buzz all afternoon. At cross, Coach was holding a flyer when we got in the locker room. He was standing, waiting. Nobody spoke. When we were all present, he walked to the middle of the room.

"I'm guessing everybody knows about this." He waved the crumpled flyer. "Admin has been talking to the police all afternoon, surveillance tapes are being reviewed. The whole works. But I want you to know. A paper like this will be stopped. But damn it . . . it's not worth wiping your butt with. If any of you are feeling disgusted or angry, use those feelings. Use them to be a better person. Kinder. More tolerant. Use those feelings to run hard. To dedicate your life to decency. The person who wrote this is sick, crazy with hate. Be glad you have a different heart. And a different life." He tore the paper up and threw it in the garbage.

While I ran, I thought about the Manifesto. And then I thought about Emily sharing what Raelene had told her. The brother made up a name for himself. And I got it. By myself. Doctor Death. I could finally see the connections, the way the story had been tying together for weeks. I didn't account for the fire, but the pets, the vandalism? It was Raelene's brother, or possibly her crazy father. I was going to find out exactly what was happening out there and then I was going to put a stop to it.

19

I HAD SAID GOOD NIGHT TO MOM, said I'd be home around ten, and gone out like I was visiting friends. Mom didn't notice my black clothes, probably wouldn't have thought anything about it if she had. I stuck my short Maglite and a screwdriver in my jeans but hoped I wouldn't need them. If they didn't have watchdogs, they probably didn't lock doors or sheds either. I planned to put my car out of sight up a dirt road I'd found a short distance east of them. If I screwed up and had to run again, I could hide in the scrub and get the car later.

The moon had cycled nearly full and the high desert ranchland glowed under a clear sky. It was final-exam quiet. I could still hear my engine ticking when I was fifty feet away. By the time I reached the crest of their hill, a breeze picked up, carrying the odor from the burial pit.

The Taurus sat to the side as usual. As soon as I saw the sets of clothes hanging on the porch, I decided to go right to the nearby shed and search it for proof, extra Manifesto flyers, anything that would link the Guru to this hate stuff or drug selling.

I had snuck to the far wall of the outbuilding and was staring at a pile of gas cans . . . *the fires* . . . when a big gray goose came around the corner and ran at me hissing and honking. *What the—?* I had an impulse to grab it, wring its neck, when I remembered I was trespassing and could get shot. I spun around and saw the porch light go on. While I ran for the Taurus, I glimpsed the skinny old man clamber out on the porch carrying what looked like a stubby shotgun. A sawed-off.

"Hold it!" he said, but I was almost there. I thought he wouldn't shoot his car. Once I got to it I would head away from the house, the Ford a shield to obstruct his line of fire. That old man couldn't be very fast.

I slid behind the sedan, got to my knees and looked though the car windows to see if he was coming after me. He had the gun ready but the stairs were giving him trouble. The goose hit me from behind and knocked me to the ground. I was trying to get hold of its neck and it was pecking knots on my face and chest. I don't know how I got to my feet but I made a loop out behind the car and took off running uphill toward the stock gate. He let loose a blast and then another. I didn't feel any pellets.

The goose quit chasing me and I was running like hell past a stunted tree when I tripped and plowed a furrow with the heels of my hands and my chin. I jumped up but somebody kicked my feet out from under me before I could take off. I tried to turn and see what was going on, but whoever it was clubbed me and all I could see was red. I curled into a ball to minimize damage in case he kept swinging.

"I told you this pigeon prick would come back."

I heard that. He hit me again and I must have passed out.

WHEN I CAME AROUND I kept my eyes closed and waited for my head to stop whirling. Waited for the pain to back off so I could think. I needed an advantage. Some guys were talking above me.

". . . out here peeping. The kid we hammered in the flop—"

"Why don't we just kill him? Megabucks says nobody knows he's here."

"Risk prison?"

"My old man will know what to do. Let's drag him back to the house."

"Hey, no offense, MDD, but your dad's nuts. You said so yourself. He'll want to convert him or some such shit, and the kid'll run and bring everybody down."

"Yeah, Einstein? Well, what the hell do I tell Dad?"

"Cinch. Tell him the punk got away but you'll take care of it tomorrow."

This was a three-guy conversation. Were there more around who weren't speaking?

The raspiest voice, the one that had suggested killing, said, "How 'bout if I crack him a couple more times and we won't have to do anything with him. He'll be a turnip."

"I like it. Might be simplest. We ought to get him off MDD's place and do him down by Laurel. Cave his head and pitch him in the river. You care, Doc?"

"I'm thinking Dad'll go mental if he doesn't get to talk to

him. Let's take him to the house first, and we can dent him up when Dad racks. Then everybody's happy."

"What about Raelene?"

"I'll go back now and have him lock her down. She could be why he's sniffing around here in the first place."

It sounded like one of them was scuffing his shoes on the gravel, but other than that it was quiet for a bit.

The last voice, the one the other called MDD or Doc, said, "Give me two minutes and then bring him."

Einstein said, "You got it."

I heard steps walking away.

"Hey, simmer down, Juley. Your chance is coming."

"Eat me."

"Go light a dog."

I could hear some wrestling near me but nobody hit the ground. I was thinking I might be able to get to my feet, but I still felt dizzy. I couldn't outrun these guys right now. Maybe after things stopped spinning. I knew I didn't have too long. I was going to get seriously damaged. And they were right, no one knew I was out here, but they couldn't know that for sure. Okay. That was my first plan. Maybe I could bluff and keep them from hurting me any more.

I was lying on my side. I risked opening my lower eye. Blurry ground in front of me. Guess they were at my back. I opened the other. The stock gate was thirty or forty yards up the hill. That put the gully in the direction of my feet. Above me I could see the branches of the tree that tripped me. Straining my eyes farther to the side I thought I could see the rear fender of a car behind tall brush. A light-colored car. Maybe it wasn't the tree that tripped me. I thought I knew who my companions were. The blonds. The punks from Durmie's room.

"Put him in the car or drag him?" The raspy voice, Juley, I thought.

"You're not going to just fungo him up to the steps?"

"Not a bad idea."

One of them gave me a middle-sized klonk on the head. I must have yelled, because Einstein said, "Sounds like you're waking him up. Let's use the car."

They picked up my shoulders and feet, carried and dropped me at the rear door. When they opened it, Einstein said, "You ride in back so he don't jackrabbit."

They lifted me in, letting me slip to the floor. The other guy slid in the seat above me and put his feet on my arms. We coasted downhill to the house. I still hadn't let them know I was awake. My head was shooting pain and I was breathing hard, bad scared. I believed them. I might not survive this.

When the car stopped rolling, they sat for a minute before both got out and closed the doors. Sounded like they walked away from the car. I got my hands under me and pushed up so I could look. The two guys were standing ten feet away, facing the house, talking to the kid I had seen before on the stool in the corner.

My head flared and I lay back. Damn it! Once again, like with Anita, I had been so stupid that things would never be the same again. Right now these guys didn't know I knew about the dogs, didn't know what I'd discovered, but they knew I'd seen the naked house and could report it . . . or did they? Maybe they thought I— My headache blazed again. Could I run now? Right now, if I got a decent start, they probably couldn't catch me. Two Bull could catch me, not these holes. But the dome light would go on if I opened the door! Would I even get a head start?

"Gabe. They're tweaked. He's psycho with the bat . . . Judd's got a gun."

I knew that voice. Crane.

"THAT'S THE FIRST TIME you knew Crane was with the twins?" Childress asked, a hard edge to her voice I hadn't heard before.

"I hadn't really spent any time with him the last month," I said.

"Thought you two were friends," she said.

"We were." *Are?* I knew I'd never see him the same way again. "We saw each other at cross but we hadn't been talking much. He was getting . . . like, bitter?" The word "sour" came to mind. "He was in a bad mood a lot, Two Bull topping him in every race when last year as a sophomore he'd been the star. So he was grumpy and his speed was . . . seemed like he was getting a little slower. I thought he was spending more time with Genelle, and I was getting more and more involved in what was happening with Durmie and Raelene. I mean, I didn't know they were connected—"

"You didn't." Childress looked away.

I could hear it: she didn't believe me.

Kosich changed the subject. "I get it about the Ray girl and

Emily. You were desperate for another girlfriend. But why did you care so much about Williams if you weren't involved in the whole scam?"

"Durmie . . . I, uh, I admired him."

Kosich pinched the bridge of his nose like I was giving him a headache.

Childress looked back and forth between the two of us. Interested bystander now.

"Durmie . . . I've had things happen in my life. Knocked me pretty flat. Dad leaving. Getting killed. I spent a fairly long time not caring if *I* kept living. Not even sad, really, more like numb. Meeting Durmie, here's a guy that's mentally ill, practically broke, living in a toilet, but most of the time he's busy, happy, always got something going. I . . . he amazed me. He was, is, like an example of grabbing life by the nuts and doing your thing in spite of . . . in spite of . . ." I didn't know how to finish. I hadn't exactly known I thought this about Durmie. I just knew I liked him and didn't want anyone to make things worse for him than they already were.

"So you were telling about being at Ray's house and finding Crane in the front seat," Childress said, getting us back on track.

"Yeah," I said, noticing how I sounded. Drained. For a second I flashed on the last few days. How much had happened, how my head kept aching, how alone I'd gotten. Sleep welled up, washing over me like a warm bath. I forced those thoughts out of my mind. "Okay, yeah, Crane was in the front seat. Hadn't said a word up till then. Had heard or watched them beat me and hadn't said a word."

20

I PUSHED UP AGAIN to look at the front seat. Crane was slouching against the door, looking at me, his face saggy. He was wasted.

"What . . ." I couldn't formulate the question.

"Yeah. Sorry—"

The back door ripping open startled us.

"Get out." The blond spike-haired kid stood there.

I was divided against myself. Part of me wanted to lunge at him, take everybody by surprise, and start running. Part of me wanted to wait until I felt a little stronger and I could maybe dive out a house window and sprint while they were still inside. They would come out night-blind and I'd have a better chance. The hesitation decided for me. Spiky raised a bat and I climbed out before he used it.

"Wait there!" he said into the car.

Crane didn't say anything. Rested his head on his side window and closed his eyes.

The punk pointed toward the porch with the bat.

The first thing I noticed was that the clothes were missing, gone from the hooks. Did the blonds not know about the na-kedness? Einstein—Judd, according to Crane—and the thin, dark-haired kid I had seen naked, Homer Ray, stood on the porch, waiting.

Homer opened the front door and stepped out of my way as I walked inside, Juley behind me. Judd and Homer followed, closed the door.

I flinched at the click of the lock and hoped no one noticed. Didn't want them to know I was spooked. The big window I'd spied through before was to my right; the ground, I remembered, was about six feet below it. There was a small window immediately to my left, by the door, but the way it was framed I didn't think I could jump through it. Raelene was nowhere to be seen. The curtain between the living room and the kitchen area was pulled shut. *Lock her down?*

The dad was sitting in his chair in the middle of the front room at a slight angle to the big window. Khaki clothes, stringy hair. I followed his gaze to the TV in the corner on my right. He was watching a videotape of himself speaking. The same sound I heard here before. The guy on the tape was actually sort of handsome, younger and much more vital-looking. He wasn't catching the news! He was reliving his glory days. Pitiful.

Homer picked up the remote from the small table beside his dad's chair and shut the TV off. The dad blinked his eyes two or three times as if that might transport him back to the present. He turned his head slowly and looked up at me.

He's sick, I thought again. I mean I knew he was sick in the head, but he looked like he had AIDS or something. He was barely holding on.

He gestured with his head, indicating he wanted me to stand in front of him.

I did. I heard the look-alikes moving as well, staying behind me. Too bad. That put the big window at my back and the blonds directly in my way. Homer and the side table were to the right of the Guru's chair as I faced him. To the left, over his shoulder, I could see the curtain. I might be able to sprint through that and out a back door. Homer and the Guru would partially block Judd's shot if he raised his pistol.

That reminded me, where was the sawed-off? It hadn't been on the TV. I scanned the bookcases. Nope, and the old man wasn't holding it in his lap. I realized I could only see his right hand resting on his knee. He kept the other down between the chair and the side table. I didn't think the son had it, but I couldn't remember if I'd seen the back of his pants, where some people carry a short gun.

Okay, maybe it was time to make a break. I don't know if it was my headache but I was nauseated. What if I started to run and threw up instead? Or maybe that was just the way it felt when you got dead scared. I looked at my feet. I was on the rug but it was anchored by the old man's chair. I didn't think it would slip when I sprinted.

The son's movement broke my concentration. He put the remote back on the end table and stood by his dad. Next to the remote there was a clear tumbler halfway full with a brown liquid. Maybe strong tea, maybe medicine, maybe liquor. I couldn't smell it over the odor of body funk and rancid laundry that came from the man. I studied the Guru. His eyes were red-rimmed and bloodshot, but they were focused. His lips looked stuck shut with yellowish matter. I thought his hand was trembling but I didn't want to take my eyes off his face and make sure. I had never been physically near anyone this strange. He could have said anything and I wouldn't have been surprised. Like maybe "shoot him," or something in Swahili.

But he did surprise me.

"Welsh? Black Irish? Maya? You look like her boy."

Maya was my mother's name. My mother's name.

"Maya . . ." he said again. "I don't know what name she took. What is it?"

I couldn't find my voice.

A bat poked me in the back.

"James?" I said. It came out like a croak.

He looked up to the ceiling, remembering. He pursed his lips.

"She . . . she was quite a woman. Bright." He shook his head gently side to side. "Tongue like a razor. And fun. All that energy!" He closed his eyes.

After a moment he looked at me again. "What are you doing here? Tonight? . . . At all?"

God! Wasn't that the ten-million-dollar question?

The house was quiet except when a sporadic wind whopped against it, whining through the cracks like an engine with the clutch pushed in. The rafters or joists would groan. None of us made a sound.

Another poke with the bat.

I wanted to shock him. Get a rise out of him. Get back on more level footing.

"I wanted to date your daughter," I said. "She and I have class together. I asked her out. She said she couldn't. I followed her out here to see why. I saw the clothes on the hook. I saw how you make them go around naked."

I could hear weight shifting and intakes of breath behind me. Looked like the blonds hadn't known that about their good doctor. Homer was blushing, clearly embarrassed.

The old man's face crinkled with its excuse for a smile.

"No," he said, "you sure couldn't date my daughter. That would be incest."

My headache flashed. And my shoes were pinching. That's what was the matter. My feet actually itched. Maybe I had athlete's foot. I couldn't follow the conversation. But I could still run. I should run. Right now.

". . . observe the classics here. The nude body is appreciated. Adored. Until adulthood arrives, and then classics must finally be set aside and the new life lived. Michelangelo, Botticelli, they knew, and we, we have sadly forgotten how beautiful the human form is. Can be. Will be forever." His eyes closed and his voice gained a richer timbre as he spoke.

I listened in spite of myself.

"But more," he continued, "there is verse, rhetoric, declamation. We cherish architecture, painting, poetry."

He was warming up, getting louder, giving what I was certain was a memorized talk.

"We allow the light of aesthetics to govern our household. There is richness here that cannot be wholly circumscribed, that cannot be easily assimilated. Thus do we homeschool. Thus do we make our way independent of the sadly pedestrian society which surrounds us."

By this point his voice had grown soft. He had become more animated during this speech but seemed to lose stamina toward the end.

I couldn't explain it. The more he spoke, the angrier I became. Every word a jab, a goad. But I wasn't bleeding. I was burning. I wanted words of my own to incinerate him, to reduce him to ash, to absolutely annihilate his half-baked patronizing smile.

"Right! So in honor of Plato you killed your neighbors' pets and let them rot in the gully up the hill. You bestowed the classical love of beauty on your children by adoring them right into child abuse. You created such a horrible ugly scene that everyone who ever cared for you has fled with no forwarding; so ugly that unstable and homeless people fear your viciousness. And to kick off your reign of terror, you lit the Rims on fire. Where is your fiddle, you obscene—"

"*Shut up!* Shut up!" Homer shouted me silent, screaming and pounding the air with his hands. "Shut up!" one last time, and then, again, there was quiet. The walls echoed but maybe that was the wind.

The father turned his head to his boy.

"What does he mean?" he asked.

142

Homer stood facing his father, his eyes squeezed shut, his hands fists, his face now bloodred, lit by the floor lamp behind the chair.

"My friends," the boy began, nodding in the direction of the brothers, "my friends were helping me create a world of pure forms. A place where more people would think like we do . . . We were experimenting." Eyes stayed closed.

"Lighting fires? Killing pets?"

"That . . . uh, that was mostly their idea to get people's attention, to uh, to create a climate for change. You talked about that. You know. You have to create a climate for change so dull people can open their eyes. Can see. Can start to emit the light." His eyes came open as he said this. "We were just investigating. Like doing research. Nobody really got hurt. Really. A couple of dumb dogs. Grovel around for their masters. Pathetic. Uh, it wasn't really my idea. Judd said—"

But he never got to finish what Judd said. His speech was stopped by an explosion as somebody behind me, Judd, I think, shot him. Had he been aiming for the father? In one motion Sun Ray's left arm rose from where it had been out of sight on the far side of his chair and he fired the sawed-off, both barrels, past my right side into Judd, who flew away with the impact. I turned to watch and saw Juley raising his bat. No way! I tackled him and we were rolling on the floor until Raelene came in from the curtained area, I think, and hit Juley in the head with a fire extinguisher, of all things, and he was done for the night.

The red metal bottle clunked on the floor next to me and rolled a half turn to a stop.

I don't remember any other sound, nothing, until the sheriffs came, accompanied by a Billings cop who helped me to my feet and gave me his arm as he walked me outside to the ambulance. A familiar cop. A man I realized I now knew as Kosich.

21

STAYED IN THE HOSPITAL THAT NIGHT. You guys know that. Concussion. I was lucky." Did Childress come to the hospital? Did Kosich wait till my exam was over, come to my room to check on me later? I couldn't remember. Mom stayed the night. I'm sure about that.

THE NEXT MORNING I ASKED HER.

She had been sitting, dozing on and off by the window for several hours. I had registered her presence as I fuzzed in and out but we hadn't spoken. I woke more completely to dreary winter sunlight and lay quiet, watching her. Wondering.

Her book had fallen to her lap, caught by her skirt, and her mouth was parted as she slept. Perhaps she felt my gaze. For whatever reason, she opened her eyes, saw me looking at her, and sat upright in the chair. The book clattered to the floor and she seemed relieved to take her eyes off me to locate it and pick it up. When she straightened again she kept her eyes on the book's spine, as if the title would become important soon. She realized what she was doing and looked at me again.

My head ached in waves, sometimes making the light seem too intense, and I put my hand to my forehead to still the pain and help shade the glare. I had to start. "You . . . why . . . you never told me about the commune." Another wave, but I was not going to put this off.

"I, your dad and I—" Her voice was rough from sleep and she cleared her throat. "Your father and I followed Vernon, Sun, out from California. We met him when he was still a professor at Cal Tech. He was . . . special. Brilliant."

"He was a weirdo creep!" The yell sent a spear through my head.

Mom didn't move. Didn't blink.

"Ugly, crazy . . ." I ran out of gas.

"I heard," she said. "I understand—"

"You don't understand anything!" The spear again. I couldn't keep doing that. Had to keep my mouth shut. Let her talk. *Bitch.* I'd never put that word to my mother. I shut my eyes to reduce the throbbing.

AFTER A MINUTE OR SO SHE STARTED AGAIN. "Before you were born, say twenty years ago, Sun Ray was the most amazing person I had ever met. Able to inspire people. Able to articulate ideas about goodness and love that actually motivated people to live differently. To live better. To take care of each other—"

"To sleep with anything that moved."

Mom didn't respond right away. I could hear her bending for her purse. I was guessing Kleenex but I wasn't going to look at her right then.

"Yes," she said, more softly. "Back then it wasn't so . . . relationships, some relationships were more open. At the community many of us expressed our love, uh, in a lot of ways. Yes, physically, sometimes with more than one . . . with someone other than our spouse. And we took in strays. I don't mean that condescendingly. There weren't the social support programs we have now in this area, and we cared for people who had no money, no other place to stay. The community held classes, sponsored food drives—"

"I don't care about that." It was true. I didn't give a damn what that place did. I cared what she did. What Dad did. "Did you do things with Sun Ray? Just tell me and then leave me alone."

Silence. And then I thought she might be crying, but I'd be damned if I'd open my eyes. She didn't deserve to be looked at.

"Yes," she said. "I'm so sorry you had to find out this way."

That was too much. "You're sorry!" I was trying to sit up now. I wanted to hit her. "Pretty goddamn late to be sorry, isn't it?"

A nurse hustled in. Must have heard me. She rushed to the bed, cut off my view of Mom, and put her hands gently but firmly on my shoulders. "Settle down," she said with a really soothing voice. "Upset makes it worse. Keeps you hurting. Lie back. Be still. Just for a minute."

She stayed in the same position, blocking me from Mom, till I lay back and closed my eyes again.

I heard Mom moving behind her. Heard metal, a zipper or a button, brush something as she picked up her coat.

"Gabe. I don't want to leave, but I will so you can get some rest. I'll be back soon enough. We'll continue this talk."

I heard her shoes clicking away and then silence. Only my breathing. And finally the bed shifting as the nurse took her hands off me and left the room.

WHEN I WOKE AGAIN Mom was back in the chair. She didn't look good.

"Ask the nurse for some water," I said.

"I'll get it." She rose and poured from the stupid little plastic pitcher.

My head still ached but it was duller. "Am I Sun . . . is Sun Ray my real father?" Just the words ratcheted the pain higher.

"Do you want to wait a little longer? Till you feel better?"

That was a stupid question. She didn't used to be so stupid.

"Okay," she said. The book was gone and her hands were in her lap. She looked at them for a moment and then at me. "Yes," she said. "Sun Ray. He could have been."

I heard her. I heard the words.

"Or your dad could have been. I know you won't understand this, but at the time it didn't really matter. We all loved each other. We all loved you. It was about love. It wasn't about ownership or DNA."

THE INTERROGATION OF GABRIEL JAMES

I yelled then. And cursed her. And called her names and the pain was blinding and people came in the room and I'm not sure exactly what happened after that.

On and off I was dreaming. I was in an avalanche, tumbling, and rocks would hit me or I'd slide into them. I couldn't tell if I was upside down. But sometimes it would be quiet and I would see things that looked like blurry signs or lighted messages drifting toward me. I couldn't make them clear enough to read. And shadows that might have been Raelene or Homer. And I became tangled in Sun Ray's beard, greasy, smelly, and I had to run but I couldn't get up. Couldn't anyone hear me?

I WOKE AGAIN, damp and exhausted. When my eyes focused I saw it was night. I tried to sit up but there was a strap across my chest. Maybe they thought I was going to fall out of bed, maybe they thought I was crazy. My movement awoke Mom and she got up immediately and left the room. Came back in seconds with a different nurse who unhitched the strap and asked me if I was hungry.

At different times that night Mom would tell me more. But I was distant. Removed. I can't explain it. She said things I couldn't stand but I didn't react much. Didn't go batshit. Maybe they'd given me something that evened me out.

Mom admitted that Raelene and Homer and I might be related. She said it was reasonable for me to be very angry and to blame her for not telling me earlier. She said she'd given it a lot of thought, talked it over with Dad before their divorce, and they'd agreed it was best to wait. She said this year, this summer, as

I had seemed more mature, as I seemed to be recovered from the divorce and Dad's death, that she'd talked it over with a therapist she respected. She wanted to do the right thing. The best thing. But she didn't know what it was. The therapist recommended waiting. Waiting until I graduated from college. But now events had decided otherwise.

I couldn't say how I felt listening to her. My skull would throb from time to time, but I didn't push the information away. I heard it. And if anything maybe I thought I'd store it and deal with it later. Later. When I had feelings again and my mother didn't seem like a complete stranger. I swear, as I lay there, she didn't look the same. She could have been anybody.

22

THE NEXT MORNING, or maybe it was Saturday, Mom told me that Homer Ray was dead. I thought he might be. I hadn't seen or heard him again once the commotion started. Judd's bullet hit an artery, so Homer bled to death. Judd himself was killed instantly by the shotgun blast. Justifiable homicide? I didn't realize it at the time, but while we were talking, the State Cross-Country Meet was beginning in Butte. Mom didn't mention it and I didn't remember.

Officer Childress visited that same morning, or noon, as an orderly was taking away my lunch tray. She introduced herself and told me the blond guys were twins, Judd and Jules Dersch. She said that Jules was in juvenile hall, charged with hate crimes, possession, and sales. No bail. Might not get any. District Attorney was filing a brief to try him as an adult.

She said that Crane had been arrested and charged: possession with intent to sell. That Wednesday night he'd been taking Klonopin for the first time, mixed with his mom's own prescription for Percodan. He'd actually slept through the shooting.

The officers found him passed out in Judd's car with the Perc and packets of benzos and oxy in his pocket. The glove compartment had more, along with tabs of the steroid Methanabol and a bottle of Adderall. They found a ziplock of pot under the seats.

Childress asked me if I knew about the steroids.

"Crane, you mean? We never really talked about that. I mean, we wondered maybe if they make you run faster," I said. "I didn't know he had any."

At that point she told me I was being considered a material witness and that I would be released from the hospital but that I had to remain available because we would need to speak officially very soon. She said her office and the D.A. were gathering information prior to further charges.

I wanted to ask if that meant me. I should have asked then, before I got in this room with the recorder.

"SO YOU GUYS KNOW THE REST," I said, putting my hands on the table, feeling like it was time to get up. "You were there that night," I said to Kosich. "How'd you get there so quick?"

Kosich paused, looked at his watch. After a moment he turned to Childress. "We done here?"

"I don't know," Childress said, looking at him to better read the intention behind the question. After a few seconds she turned off the recorder.

"Your mother gave me the card with the license number," Kosich said.

"The Chevy? The number I found in Durmie's room?"

"The Ford," he said. He shook his head. "I should have run it sooner. It matched the Taurus that Homer drove."

I had trouble letting go of the Chevy. "Homer? They used his car to sell drugs?"

Kosich shrugged.

"Durmond Williams saw something," Childress said, "knew something about Homer Ray. Might have been the vandalism, might have been the pets. Could even have been the fire. That big Rims fire. That's probably why the twins were looking in Williams's room. The only reports about drug sales we got"—she looked in her pocket notepad—"were from a homeless guy called, uh, Lucius. He said it was a yellow Chevy."

"Why did Mom give the card to you? And not to Childress or somebody else?"

"We've known each other for a long time. She—" Kosich stopped talking for a minute or more.

Watching him, hands in his pockets, thinking, I couldn't understand what was happening.

Childress stayed quiet. Leisurely looking back through the information in her spiral pad.

"Your mother told you, right?" Kosich asked.

"Told me . . ." Now I wanted to stand. Stand and leave. But would they stop me?

"About the commune," Kosich said. "About being a member?"

I waited.

"I, uh, I . . ." Kosich rubbed his hands. Looked to Childress, as if for advice.

I couldn't believe it. The Lump was nervous. Off-balance and bothered about something. *Was that why he'd been so disconnected and erratic today?* He was my mom's age. Was—?

"Why don't we talk about this later?" Childress said, picking up the Stetson, putting it on, adjusting it in the mirror.

The mirror. Someone was watching us. Childress was cuing Kosich not to say anything here. She flicked on the recorder again. "Let's finish up here," she said.

Kosich nodded. Turned his back on the mirror, checked his watch again.

"So what did you know about Sun Ray? Did he . . . was he physical with Raelene? Or the brother?" Childress asked.

Physical. She didn't mean spank. She meant sexual. I didn't want to think about that.

"I don't know," I said. "The Guru passed it off as some kind of philosophical deal. I think the no-clothes was a total secret. I'm pretty sure the twins didn't know. I bet Homer didn't want anyone to know."

"Did what's-her-name say anything?"

"Emily couldn't even stand to hear about it. I'm sure she wouldn't ask that sort of thing, and Raelene wouldn't tell."

Childress chewed on the tip of her ballpoint.

"Am I under arrest?" Finally. I had to know.

Kosich turned to look at me. Face blank.

Childress took the pen from her mouth, hesitated, put it in her pocket. "Obstruction," she said. "If you'd come to us earlier with what you suspected—"

"I gave you the license number."

She looked to Kosich.

He nodded.

She shut off the recorder. "Give us a minute," she said.

23

THEY RELEASED ME late in the afternoon. Leaving the Annex, my headache blazed when the sunlight hit my eyes but I made it to my car and walked around it, lowering the windows. I needed fresh air. And quiet. I sat behind the steering wheel without starting the engine.

Childress had told me that, so far, Sun Ray was charged with manslaughter, terrorism, and arson, with other charges pending. Ray was denying knowledge of the fire, the dogs, and the vandalism. I could believe him, remembering the way he looked at his son just before Judd shot. And I couldn't imagine an ex–classics professor writing the Manifesto. Way too dumb. Plus, I remembered listening to Judd and Jules and Homer talk about what to do with me. I believed, together, they were capable of any degree of violence.

According to Childress, Ray's physical exam in jail led to further tests that showed he had late-stage pancreatic cancer. The continuing investigation, let alone the trial, could last past his life expectancy. Currently, Ray was refusing medical care and all visitors, and had asked his court-appointed attorney to help him draw up a quick will leaving everything to Raelene.

Raelene had left immediately after the funeral, left town the same day to live with an aunt, her dad's only sister, somewhere in Oregon. I guess anything would be better than staying here after all that information broke following the shooting and the sheriff's investigation.

Of course I'd missed State. So did Crane. Me, hospital, Crane, juvie. Danny Two Bull won by a furlong. Set a record. Sparks got sixth and our team came in tenth out of fourteen. If I'd been there and run my best time to date, I might have placed as low as twentieth and we'd have moved up to eighth or so. If Crane had been there, we might have won the whole thing.

I hadn't visited Crane, yet. His warning that night might have saved my life, but I couldn't deal with the deceit or the drugs-to-run-better thing. Last summer we'd experimented a couple of times with his mom's scripts. I guess I was lucky. I didn't like the way I zombied out on downers. Crane said he kind of liked it, believed it might help him run with less leg pain. I thought he would give up the idea. Instead, looks like it started him thinking about other additives. Might never have done it if Two Bull hadn't started smoking him every meet.

So I didn't know what to say to Crane. At this moment, I hated him. Hated him. He'd been right there, when they were talking about killing me. Can drugs totally erase a friendship?

And I felt . . . can you feel guilty but not exactly responsible? Should I have known? Wib visited me in the hospital before I was released. I'll talk to Wib. Get his take on the whole thing. If I ever let it go, it won't be soon.

I bet Two Bull was relieved to find out who was behind the attacks. I imagine he was glad to have it stopped and to get on with running and school, quit watching for what was coming next. At least I hoped it was stopped. Homer and the twins had gotten twisted by their sicko parents. Took it out on everybody else. There's a lot of messed-up families. There's a lot more kids out there waiting to go off.

I knew why I didn't want to start my car. I didn't want to drive home and face Mom. Mom in a cult. Sleeping around. Getting together with that creep. Doesn't know if I'm my dad's son. I don't know what to say to her, don't know what I'll do. I keep flashing on driving my old Land Cruiser right into the house. Bash down the walls.

I knew the commune was a long time ago. Seventeen years. But could I trust her again? What other secret was she keeping for my own good? Could I forgive her? That was probably the right thing to do. Easy to say.

I tried to imagine what else Mom would tell me. Yeah, things were different then. Monogamy wasn't such a big deal. It was really like a big family, mixing the good with the bad. Sun Ray was different. He made people think about their lives, their beliefs. The commune did good things for the community. Right.

And Kosich. Probably there with Mom and now a cop.

What was that about? The question made me queasy. Hope to god *he's* not my real father. Would he tell me if I asked him? How would I ever know? They don't even know. How sick is that? DNA? I couldn't imagine going through with that. I glanced back at the Annex.

Kosich stood on the steps outside the front door, looking at me.

24

MOM WAS WAITING WHEN I GOT HOME.

"We still need to talk," she said.

"*You* need to talk," I said. "I don't need to hear. I've already thought about what you'll say."

"Let me explai—"

"Did Kosich call you? Talk to you about Sun Ray? About me?"

She didn't have to answer. I could see it in her eyes. But I waited.

"Yes."

"How long have you known him?"

"Twenty years or more."

"He was with you and—" I'd been going to say Dad but the word stuck in my craw. "Did he live at Dell?"

"At first, yes, until his wife moved back to Missoula."

I was having trouble listening, having trouble standing still. What had Crane told me? About hitting a wall? Have to miss the stud or you'll break your hand.

"He moved into Billings then. I lost track of him for several years. A while ago he brought a street person to the Center for stabilizing. I didn't recognize him at first. He's put on a lot of weight."

Yeah, so what. "What did he say when he called?"

"It was the night of the shootings. He said you'd been out at Dell, that you'd been clubbed and that they were taking you by ambulance to Deaconess Hospital."

"Is that all?"

"I was in a big hurry when he told me. He used the word 'concussion.'"

"What else?"

"He asked me if you'd ever spent any time with Phillip Shay."

My stomach dipped. Shay, the guy Kosich had talked about. The pedophile. "Shay was Sun Ray's buddy?"

"One of the first who joined. The commune. Became Sun's accountant, business manager really. I think he moved in with Sun and the kids when their second mom left, when they were young. He was the last member to leave. I don't know what happened to him."

Right. According to Kosich he was in prison. "So did I?"

"Spend time with Phillip? No. Neither your dad . . . we didn't like him. Didn't trust him. There was something off about him."

"What else did he ask?"

"Kosich . . . I have trouble thinking of him as a policeman. For years I knew him as—"

"I don't care!" I enjoyed cutting her off, hurting her feelings. Ugly. But true.

She started again. "He asked if you could have done any of the vandalism: the fire, the pets. I told him I thought you were out of town when the fire started. That you'd never shown any cruelty to people or animals. I said you were a good—" but she choked up and couldn't finish.

I waited her out. Tears weren't going to derail me.

She looked around for something to wipe her eyes, wound up using her hands. "You're just like me," she said.

I wasn't ready for that.

"You want things to be right. Want to help people. You stick your nose in their business and don't know what to do with what you find out. Sometimes you see you're doing more harm than good."

I didn't have to stand here. Listen to this. Didn't owe her anything. Didn't want her excuses.

She kept on. "You hold things to yourself. Things you should tell someone else. You always think you know what's best so you don't get the perspective you need. Your secrecy causes problems."

"Hey!" I wanted to break something. A window. Throw a lamp. I could. Her crap was all over the living room. "You told me I'm not your whole life. There at Smokey's? Okay! I get it! You're not my whole life either. I don't have to tell you everything!" My eyes blurred with tears, but I was on a roll. "You do what you want. I do what I want! No big deal. That's the way life is. I don't even know if you're really my mother. I could just be one of the commune brats you walked away with!" I had to stop to get a breath.

I wasn't going to look at her. Didn't want to see her. Maybe ever. Maybe I would walk out like Dad—but her sob drew my eyes. At some point in the day she'd put on a little makeup. It was sliding down her face now and she didn't raise her hands to mop it. I had never seen her like this. Not even when Dad left.

I wasn't like her. *I wasn't!* Let her cry herself to death. Where was that vase her mom gave her? On the mantel. I grabbed it and threw it in the fireplace. It broke in a thousand pieces. I knew how that felt.

SOMETIME LATER I REALIZED I HADN'T LEFT. I was sitting on the floor, leaned up against Dad's old chair. My face itched from salt streaks, my collar was damp. Had I been asleep? I didn't know. The sun was low and the gray dusk barely gave the room any light. Mom was on the couch, across from me, head in her hands, quiet, still.

I had to get away. Get out. See the sky. I grabbed my jean jacket and headed for my car, but stopped as I got to the driveway. In the car I'd be closed in. I didn't want it. I walked instead. Not usual for me, I either drove or ran, but right then I needed room to move.

I walked toward Veterans Park, a half block west of my house. I could already picture the huge sunken lawn the city would fill with water in a few weeks for the winter skating rink. I could picture the adobe brick recreation cottage with the cast-iron stove where Wib and I would take off our skates and warm our feet after horsing around the rink till our ankles were numb. I could picture the metal push-me merry-go-round just up the hill where I'd once made myself so dizzy I heaved on a sixth grade girl I had wanted to impress. But I couldn't picture, didn't picture, the man I saw bending over the garbage cans at the curb nearest the baseball diamond. Durmie.

He had his back to me.

"Hey! Hey! Mr. Williams!" I was yelling. "You need some help?"

Durmie looked up, over to the infield, over to the rec cottage, before turning enough to see me. "Hey, yourself, Teach," he said, rearranging his face from a frown of concentration to a smile. "You wanta give me a hand here? I'm coldin' up and my back is spazzin'."

I kept myself from running, but I would have flung my hat off if I'd worn one. "What the hell? What are you doing here?" It didn't make any sense.

"I'm taking care of bizness, Teach," he said, shaking his head like I was beyond dense. "Trying my luck, making a buck. You know me. Always workin'."

"No," I said, reaching him, clapping him on the shoulder. "I mean I thought you went to Warm Springs."

Durmie held his shoulder where I clapped him. "Hey, Teach, you got to take it easy on me. I'm not so well. Got burstitis, can't hardly lift my arm, all them needles." He looked down in the can he'd been rifling. "You give me a hand here with the bottom? I can't never nearly reach it." He stepped back from the rack of fifty-gallon containers and opened his cloth sack like Santa Claus. "You could just put 'em right in here."

Here we go again, but I was glad to see him standing and really didn't mind. "Okay, I'll pitch in, but what happened? How come you're out and about?"

"Well, I got the news. You know that whosit? The brown-headed one, stacked like a deck?"

I wasn't putting it together.

"The one from day shift? She kinda liked me special. Leanin' over, rubbin' me, talking pretty?"

"The nurse? The Charge Nurse? At the hospital?"

"You betcha. But don't be gettin' ideas. You already got yers."

I didn't, but I didn't want to get into it. "The Charge Nurse gave you what news?"

"That you busted 'em! That's what. Shot 'em up, roped em, stuck 'em in the tank." He was clearly proud of me, smiling at me, but at the same time nodding at the garbage receptacles that I was supposed to be emptying of cans. "They's probably a bunch all the way down," he said.

"Durmie, I didn't bust—"

"You clean up the town, I don't got to use one of my times," he said.

I wanted to understand but I didn't. "One of your times?"

"The state don't let ya just be there all the time, Teach," he said, straining to be patient. "You go now, you can't go again for a while, a few months. And the hawk is out. You see that. Janrary and Febrary are the time to be there. Chrismas if you can swing it. Presents and everthing. Got a Parker a couple of years back."

"A Parker?"

"King a the pens, Teach, you oughta know that. Don't forget that one on the side," he said, gesturing with the sack.

25

AT THE GRAVEYARD LAST SUNDAY you could look out across the hills and practically see the battlefield the Indians called Greasy Grass. History judged Custer harshly. Said that he didn't listen to his scouts; that he was vain, rash, eager to make a name for himself at anyone's expense. I'd wondered if that description fit me.

At the time, I'd also wondered how history would judge the Ray family. I imagined the father would be seen as a lunatic, a man disabled by psychedelic drugs who experienced too much personal power early on, too much isolation later. Homer would probably be pitied by some, hated by most. And with any luck, Raelene would be forgotten, left alone to heal slowly, allowed to make her way in the world.

Mom and Dad both lived at Dell. Lived a life so different I can't really understand it. Their actions had consequences that traveled into my present. And this fall things happened in our town that don't heal easily; things that make people choose up sides. In a way, from the fire on, we were all involved, all kind of nervous. Weren't we? Or is that just Typhoid Gabriel rationalizing? Wouldn't both young men still be alive if I hadn't gone out there that night?

Made me feel like running. And running and running and running.

BUT I DIDN'T RUN. When I left Durmie, I went back home. Opened the front door to the smell of tacos.

I chopped tomatoes and shredded the cheese.

Dinner was silent. After we cleaned up we went back to the living room. Mom took the couch and I got in Dad's easy chair. We didn't turn on the TV. I could see that neither of us knew what to do. Maybe wouldn't for a long time.

When the house phone rang, Mom didn't stir and I didn't answer it. After the message machine finished our greeting, Wibby's voice came on. He said Shugaart's older sister, Crystal, a junior in choir, really likes me.

ACKNOWLEDGMENTS

THIS BOOK is a collaboration and I am thankful for the help and encouragement. I appreciate my agent, Tracey Adams, her husband, Josh, and my publisher, Simon Boughton, for making this project possible. I am honored to have Wesley Adams as my editor and I am grateful for the many, many ways he has enriched the quality of this manuscript.

Three years ago, when I first started telling this story, my Billings friend-since-grade-school and fishing partner, Harry Miller, sent me maps and brought me up to date on the city. Kit Anderton and Deborah Steen read my early versions diligently and *Interrogation* benefited from their many recommendations. Michael Wyatt educated me about current cross-country strategies. Dr. Paul Swinderman gave me ongoing medical consultations pertaining to the story line. Manuel J. Garcia provided similar advice and perspective in legal areas. My daughter, Jesse, critiqued paragraphs with a keen eye, and my psychotherapist wife, Joan Pechanec, patiently read page after page,

time after time, proving that love, if not blind, can at least endure eyestrain.

While this story reflects true events, names and geography
have been hugely altered to protect anonymity. In 1993, the
city of Billings, Montana, responded wholeheartedly and pow-
erfully to an escalating series of hate crimes committed against
Jews and Native Americans in the local community. Led by
the chief of police, businesses, religious groups, the labor coun-
cil, and ten thousand local citizens joined together in declar-
ing that the racist attacks must cease. These courageous people
and the *Not in Our Town* documentary that chronicled their
action have since inspired communities across the nation and
around the world. I set my novel in Billings to join in the cele-
bration of their successful effort.

Billings is also my hometown. I graduated from Billings
Senior High and spent some of the best years of my life playing
football, making music and singing, fishing rivers, and slow-
dancing to ballads in the varnished gymnasiums that smelled
like popcorn and practice jerseys.

For consistent inspiration from my writing community,
an alphabetical THANKS to: Steve Brewer, Deborah Brodie,
Melinda Brown, Chris Crutcher, Jim Dowling, Tony D'Souza,
Kathryn Gessner, Carla Jackson, Melinda Kashuba, Robb
Lightfoot, and my man who lives his writing, Bill Siemer.